A Lesson in Love

By Linda Shenton Matchett

A Lesson in Love
By Linda Shenton Matchett

Copyright 2025 by Linda Shenton Matchett. All rights reserved.
Cover Design by: Wes Matchett
Photo Credits:
Woman in hat: Deposit Photos/Mavoimages
Man: Shutterstock/Angela Holmyard
Belton Manor: Pixabay/MemoryCatcher

ISBN: 979-8-9877458-9-2

Published by Shortwave Press

Without limiting the rights under copyright reserved above, no part of this publication may be reproduced, stored in or introduced into a retrieval system, or transmitted, in any form, or by any means (electronic, mechanical, photocopying, recording, or otherwise), without the prior written permission of both the copyright owner and the above publisher of this book.

The scanning, uploading, and distribution of this book via the Internet or via any other means without the permission of the publisher is illegal and punishable by law. Please purchase only authorized electronic editions, and do not participate in or encourage electronic piracy of copyrighted materials. Your support of the author's rights is appreciated.

This is a work of fiction. Names, characters, places, and incidents either are the products of the author's imagination or are used fictitiously. Any resemblance to actual events or persons, living or dead, is entirely coincidental.

No generative AI (Artificial Intelligence) was used in the writing of this work. The author expressly prohibits any entity from using this publication for the training of AI technologies to generate text, including without limitation technologies that are capable of generating work in the same style of genre of this publication. The author reserves all rights to license uses of this work for generative AI training and development of machine learning language models.

August 1942

Chapter One

Giggles and the hum of conversation mingled with the *clickety-clack* of the train over the rails as the behemoth rumbled away from London. Coal-saturated smoke floated past the grimy windows, blurring the familiar landscape of centuries-old buildings. Soon the towering structures would give way to cottages, then pastures and farm animals.

Isobel Turvine sighed and fanned herself with the letter she'd received last week explaining her assignment, but the motion did little to relieve the stifling air in the passenger car. She couldn't remember the last time August had been so hot. With another sigh, she shifted on the barely padded seat. What had she been thinking? She was a schoolteacher, not a common laborer. Sidewalks and congestion were what she knew, not wide-open spaces with cows, chickens, and sheep.

"Stop fidgeting." Short, stocky, and full of spice, Isobel's best friend, Margery Vincent, swatted her shoulder. "It's only a three-hour journey. We'll be there before you know it."

"That's what I'm afraid of."

"Nonsense. This is going to be an adventure." Margery grinned and flipped her white-blonde ponytail. Her blue eyes sparkled. "This is a chance to learn and be something more."

"I know, but the poster made it sound fun." Isobel waved the missive. "The letter is another whole story. Rules, regulations, and threats of dismissal if I mess up. We know nothing about planting and harvesting crops or milking cows and herding sheep. One mistake, and I'm back in London."

Left eyebrow raised, Margery glared at her. "Where is my intrepid friend who can single-handedly manage a classroom full of primary students? The recruiter said we would be trained. We're from London. They are aware we've never seen a cow except in photographs." She shrugged. "Besides, they need us. Men have left the fields for combat. The Women's Land Army is the only option they have to keep England and her troops fed."

"And I'm out of a job."

"And *we're* out of a job. Thanks to all the bombs Jerry is throwing at us, the children had to be evacuated. And with almost no students, there was no reason for the school to remain open."

"True, but there's always factory work, and it pays very well."

"Yes, and as much as I love my city, I'm happy to head somewhere I don't have to worry about being killed while I sleep."

"I'll give you that one, but we could have applied to one of the schools that has moved to the country." Isobel cringed at the whine in her voice. Since when had she become such a stick-in-the-mud? She cleared her throat. "I'm just saying that we could have searched for a job we are prepared for."

Laughter surged from the back of the car, and Margery flicked a glance toward the group. "Yes, we could have, but then we would have missed the chance to serve our troops and be part of something bigger. You hate to fail. That's what's stuck in your craw. You don't want to go down in flames. But they want us to succeed, and you're one of the most tenacious women I've ever met. You're going to be fine. No. You're going to be great."

Isobel sagged against the seat. "I am being silly, aren't I? What would I do without you?"

"First of all, you wouldn't have nearly as much fun, but I know you're worried about your brother and whether the postal service will actually forward his letters until he gets your new address."

"You're right. I don't want to lose touch or for him to worry if he doesn't hear from me. We're all we've got."

"Do you know where he is?"

"Not officially, but he mentioned haggis for breakfast, so I'm going to go with Scotland. There are several Royal Air Force bases up there." Isobel plucked at her skirt. "At least he's not overseas, but he risks his life every time he goes on a mission."

Darkness cloaked them as the train hurtled through a tunnel, the car rocking on the tracks. Isobel swallowed and her eyes closed, squeezed tightly. *One. Two. Three. Four. Five.* Margery fumbled for her hand and laced their fingers together, yet remained mute. Always the supporter, she didn't make fun of Isobel's claustrophobia.

A lifetime later, Margery released her hand indicating it was safe for Isobel to open her eyes. As if the moment had never occurred, Margery picked up the conversation. "What I'm looking forward to most is learning how to drive a tractor. Can you imagine rumbling down the field on one of those monsters?" She held up her arm, bent her elbow, and fisted her hand, then poked at the muscle in her upper arm. "This might be flab now, but wait until the end of the season. You won't recognize me."

Isobel snorted a laugh. Her friend always knew how to pull her from a blue mood. "And I'll be your wingman. We'll be quite a team. And frankly, if I'm working in the fields, I won't be trying to wrestle milk from a cow or herd sheep. But I'm anxious to see the house. Some of these manors are eight hundred to a thousand square meters or more. And the history of them goes back centuries. The architecture and the furnishings will be magnificent."

"Perhaps, but what makes you think the old codger will let us land girls live in his posh house? No. We'll be relegated to the servants' quarters or the stables most likely."

"Either way, they'll be nicer than my three-story walk-up in the East End."

"For sure." Margery crossed her arms. "He must be desperate to turn his fields over to a bunch of women."

"His place might be one the government requisitioned. Don't you remember the recruiter talking about that? Not everyone is offering their mansion."

"Hmm. That could make for an interesting situation. When this is all over, you should write a book about it. Future generations will want to know about what happened, and we'll be at the forefront."

Isobel tilted her head and rubbed her jaw in mock arrogance. "Yes, and Oxford University Press will publish it. I'll go on a worldwide tour, and you can be my assistant."

Margery jabbed her with an elbow. "Stranger things have happened."

"You have a very active imagination."

"So I've been told." Margery wrinkled her nose. "Now, tell me about this book of yours. It won't need to be long. We'll have one season, then the war will be over by Christmas."

"Not hardly." Isobel's stomach tightened. "Hitler has taken on Russia, and now the Americans have joined the fight."

"But Midway went well. The Japanese are on the defensive in the Pacific."

"Have you always been this naïve?"

Poking out her lower lip, Margery said, "I prefer to think of myself as an optimist."

"Well, I'm a realist, and I believe we have a long, hard fight ahead of us."

A Lesson in Love

Chapter Two

Surrounded by crates in the mahogany-paneled room, Gavin Emerson stared out the floor-to-ceiling windows at the rolling hills. The lawn surrounding the Baroque-style manor home was a bit bedraggled, and the distant meadows overgrown with brush. Like everyone else, the earl had lost most of his staff to the war effort. Had he contributed the estate to the government, or had the authorities come calling?

No matter the reason, Galvin's school was the lucky recipient. Plenty of space for classrooms and boarding the boys who would arrive in the next few days, as well as outdoor space for recreation. He didn't have nearly enough teachers, so would have to conduct classes himself in addition to being headmaster.

He'd already toured the property and learned some of its history. The earl had been surprisingly frank during their walk, sharing stories about several ancestors who'd been less than honorable as well as his own mother, who'd alternated between odd and mad as a hatter. He'd chosen not to marry to prevent passing a potential bad gene. Sad.

With a sigh, Gavin raked his fingers through his hair and turned toward the nearest crate. He pried open the lid, the puckered scar tissue on his upper arm protesting the pressure. Grunting, he stifled the urge to toss the crowbar, instead laying it on the desk. He rifled through the stacks of textbooks, one-handed, then grabbed a sheet of paper and scribbled the list of titles, before inserting the page inside the crate. A secretary would have been nice to help with some of the administrative functions, but he'd been told there was no money for such a luxury. Ha. A luxury. How was he supposed to properly run an educational institution with a handful of instructors close to or past retirement age and no clerical support?

"Moaning to yourself won't get the job done, old man." He bent over another crate. "Just get to it."

"That can't be good. You're talking to yourself already."

Gavin straightened and pivoted toward the door. "Alastair, you devil, when did you arrive?" He threaded his way through the crates and shook his best friend's hand. "You're just in time to help with sorting and distributing the textbooks."

"Och, that explains the conversation. I know how much you love this sort of task." His Scottish brogue was music to Gavin's ears. "If I'da known, I'da shown up a wee bit later."

"Well, it's too late to back out now, isn't it?"

Tall and lanky, Alastair patted his thin midsection. "Or I could find the kitchen and scare up some food. The train ride down from Glasgow left much to be desired, and I haven't eaten anythin' since breakfast."

"We'll have to remedy that, won't we?" Gavin snickered as he clapped his friend on the shoulder, then motioned toward the door. "I can't have you fainting and falling into the crates. I'm sure we can find something to fill that hollow stomach of yours."

"This is quite the place you've managed to find."

"Not me, the Ministry of Works, but I am grateful. As you'll see, it's somewhat worn but serviceable. The house must be more than a thousand square meters, and the earl said he owns over twelve hundred acres."

"Impressive."

Gavin led Alastair through the house, their footsteps echoing on the gleaming wooden floors as they tramped down the corridor. Food and supplies had been delivered three days ago, but the cooks wouldn't arrive until tomorrow, so he and the staff were on their own for meals. Not that he was much of a chef, but he could put together a decent sandwich.

They entered the kitchen, and Alastair let out a whistle as he ran his finger along the butcher-block island in the huge room. "Goodness! This is bigger than my flat. I think I'm going to like it here."

With a chuckle, Gavin motioned to the three-meter table. "Have a seat while I find up some food."

Alastair dropped into one of the dozen chairs surrounding the table. "I guess this is where the servants took their meals, eh? Must be nice."

"I don't know. The earl seemed, I don't know, tired. It takes a lot to manage a property this size. I wouldn't want the responsibility."

"Um, too late. You've already got the job."

Gavin paused, the knife hovering over the fragrant loaf of bread. "No, I'm just taking care of the school…staff and students. That's it." He cut four thick slices, then went to the icebox and pulled out the bowl of eggs he'd hard-boiled yesterday. He flashed a grin at Alastair. "Sorry, no bacon butty today, just mashed eggs and cheese."

"I may have to rethink my contract." Alastair sent him an exaggerated frown. "What sort of place is this where a man can't get a bacon butty. You'd think there was a shortage or something."

"Or something." Quickly assembling the sandwiches, Gavin set the plates on the table, then two glasses of water from a pitcher on the counter. He lowered himself on another of the chairs. "You'd think the last war to-end-all-wars would have been enough."

"Aye. 'Twas a bad one, wasn't it?" Alastair shook his head and picked up his sandwich. "But that Hitler is a madman, and he must be stopped. He's greedy and *craicte*, not a good combination."

"Crazy is right. What were the Germans thinking when they put him in power?"

"I dinnae think they knew what they were gettin'. Alastair took a bit of the sandwich and smiled. "Not bad."

"Thanks, but I'll stick to teaching." Gavin nibbled the sandwich. Tasty enough, but it was his third day of scrambled eggs. His culinary skills were limited, and stuffing some sort of filling between two pieces of bread was his go-to meal. Probably why he carried two extra stone around his middle. Maybe more.

Eyes twinkling, Alastair wolfed down the sandwich, then leaned against the back of the chair. "That'll do." He picked up the glass. "What's the earl like? A typical toff?"

"Not at all, which is a relief." Gavin pushed away his empty plate. "I mean, we'll keep the lads corralled, but they are boys, and who knows what sort of mischief they'll manage to get into. He'll need to be understanding, and since he's never married, he may not have been around many children. Could be a recipe for disaster. I plan to have a heart-to-heart with him."

"Mr. Emerson?" Distant footfalls sounded, and the earl's voice floated into the kitchen.

"In here, my lord." Gavin scrambled to his feet and gestured for Alastair to do the same. "In the kitchen."

A towering man with jet-black hair, despite his advanced age, Owen Flagler looked every bit the aristocrat he was. The house might be worn down, but his attire was impeccable. "What have I told you about that, young man? The name is Owen. To my mother's dismay, I've never stood on formality, so I shan't start now." His gaze slid to Alastair. "And who have we here?"

"Alastair Balfour, my lord."

"Tut, not you, too. Owen. The name's Owen."

"Might take some gettin' used to, si… Owen."

The earl tugged at his suit coat. "I meant to tell you I've agreed to contribute a portion of the land to the WLA. There shouldn't be any disruption to the school day, but the boys should be kept out of the women's hair."

Alastair cocked his head. "The WLA?"

"Women's Land Army. Where have you been?"

"In the city, sir, er, Owen. I'm from Glasgow."

"Of course. The WLA was started in thirty-nine to replace the lads in combat and to increase food production. Quite an organization. They do everything from plowing to harvesting and animal husbandry. This place will be a regular farm in a fortnight's time." He clapped his hands. "Anyway, carry on. Didn't want you to be surprised when a horde of women and a fleet of equipment rolled up the drive." He whirled and hurried from the room.

"Women's Land Army. Isn't that something?" Alastair leaned against the icebox. "Now, I've heard everything."

Gavin shrugged. "I read something about them in *The Times*. Shouldn't be a problem with the lads if we keep them busy with studies, activities, and chores."

Alastair smirked. "Nae. What could possibly go wrong, mixing schoolboys and fine-looking lassies working in the fields?"

A chill swept over Gavin. "When you put it that way…"

Chapter Three

Heart pounding, Isobel approached the front door of the manor home. It was still hard to believe the earl didn't expect her to slip in through the back door that led into the kitchen. He'd turned out to be gracious and down-to-earth, someone she might have enjoyed as a colleague if he'd been a teacher. She raised her hand to knock, and the door swung open.

"Miss Turvine, right on time." The earl bowed slightly as if she were of the peerage and not him. "Lovely to see you again. We'll begin our tour inside, then make our way to the barn and other buildings."

"Thank you." Her mouth dried, and she licked her lips. *Get a grip, Isobel.* "You have a beautiful home, my lord."

"Tut. I told you it's Owen or Mr. Flagler."

She slanted her gaze at him, his height creating the need to crane her neck. "Hardly that, but I'll do my best." Since when did an earl encourage such familiarity? Who was this man?

"Now, as you're aware, a boy's school is also using the property, but fortunately, the house has several wings, so we'll be segregating them from the space you ladies will be using for dining. I hope you're settling into the cottages."

"Yes, si—Mr. Flagler. Very comfortable and more than most of the girls and I are used to."

"No more than you deserve. You and the others will be working hard. You should have a nice place to reside."

Nice? The room she shared with Margery was nearly the size of her flat. Nice was an understatement.

He led her down a corridor, his long strides forcing her to almost trot to keep up. "The school will be using the east wing for boarding and the southeast wing for classrooms. The courtyard in the back will serve for their recreational activities."

Peeking into each of the rooms as they walked past, she forced her jaw closed so the earl didn't see her gaping like a tourist at the opulence. No, not opulence. Tastefully luxurious. Some of the rooms were painted in pastel colors; others featured wallpaper. All held antique furniture of various periods from Queen Anne and Georgian to Elizabethan. Gilded-framed artwork graced the walls. She'd read that the manor has been constructed in the late fifteen hundreds and could see evidence throughout the building.

They backtracked, then entered the southeast wing, and he motioned to a pair of rooms on either side of the corridor that had been fitted with tables and chairs. "There are nearly fifty boys, so, Mr. Emerson, the headmaster, has his work cut out for him, but I believe he's up to the task. You'll meet him at some point, but again, there will be little interaction."

Returning to the foyer, he opened the front door, and they stepped outside. Sunshine warmed their backs, and Isobel squinted at the brightness. Green fields stretched into the distance. The women would be hard-pressed to convert the meadows to fields for planting.

As they walked toward the immense barn, the earl said, "You're the only land girl I've asked to meet with me because I'd like you to be in charge. Normally, I believe the group selects their manager amongst themselves, but I was told you're older than most of the gals, and I watched you all arrive. I don't know your background, but your leadership capabilities are apparent."

"I-I am a teacher. Primary school." She clasped her trembling hands together. "I hadn't planned… That is…I just came to do my bit for the war effort. The truth is I know almost nothing about farmwork."

"Tut. You've corralled youngsters. Surely, you can do the same with a bunch of women. My mind is made up. I prefer to have you act as liaison. The ministry indicated that most of the individuals assigned here are versed in farming, so they can tell you what needs to be done, and you ensure that it happens."

They reached the barn, and she pressed her lips together. One side was filled with every tool imaginable, most of which she didn't recognize or know their purpose, as well as not one but two brand-new John Deere tractors. Did the earl have connections in America or just buckets of money to ship equipment across an ocean? The other side was divided into an open space for cows and a half-dozen stalls for horses.

He made a sweeping gesture. "The ministry managed to provide a list of implements needed for the job, so you and the gals should be set."

"You've been very generous."

Pulling out his pocket watch, he shrugged. "Not at all. Now, I must dash. I've just remembered a telephone call I need to make. The ministry also had your uniforms shipped here, and I had the crates put in the lorry so you can deliver them to the cottages." He made a vague motion toward the house. "The garage is behind the manor, and the keys to all the vehicles are in a box by the door in the kitchen. We'll meet again, my dear." He retraced their steps toward the house, his stride that of a much younger man.

Isobel shielded her eyes against the sun and watched him for a long moment. She knew nothing about the family, nor did she care to, but his treatment of her was unlike anything she'd expected. With a property of such magnitude, he was presumably rich as Croesus. Was it a novelty for him to have camaraderie with the lower classes or was his behavior genuine? She wasn't always a good judge of people, so she'd take him at face value, but wait to see what played out. No one with his amount of money would be just a regular guy.

She hiked back to the house, slipped into the kitchen, and grabbed the lorry key, its metal cool against her palm. She hadn't dared tell the earl that nearly a decade had elapsed since the last time she'd driven. The recruiter had told her not to worry, that there were plenty of non-motorized tasks, and she would have plenty of time to brush up on her driving. Her lips twisted. So much for that theory. Would her first day be her last after stripping the gears?

Hands stuffed in his pockets, Gavin paced across the floor of the huge office. Would he ever tire of the view? He'd finally sorted all the books, and the teachers arrived just in time to move them to the appropriate classrooms. Two of the men groused the entire time, and he'd had to bite his tongue to prevent from reprimanding them. They weren't wrong in their complaints that they were instructors and not laborers, but the war had taken every young and able-bodied man. The school didn't have the luxury of a custodial staff. Should he tell the teachers they were lucky they weren't responsible for cooking?

Huffing out a breath, he stopped at the windows and stared across the lush meadows. Interspersed by hedgerows, the gently rolling hills would soon be torn up to reveal rich, dark earth. London-born and bred, he hadn't left the city except for college. He knew nothing about raising food, but did the government really believe a cadre of women could handle back-breaking farmwork? It was one thing to be a farmwife and feed chickens or milk a few cows, but to drive tractors and sow acres of vegetable seeds, and then harvest the produce?

He shook his head and watched a bird soar overhead in the cloudless robin's-egg-blue sky. The group was already getting a late start. They should have been here in the spring, but perhaps the earl had only just offered his place. More likely, miles of red tape involved in determining the property's use had slowed the decision to a crawl. Loud voices sounded in the hallway outside his closed door. Probably Stillwell and Martin arguing over something petty. Those two would be the death of him.

Finally getting a headmaster appointment had seemed like a dream come true. Now, it seemed more like a nightmare. Granted, the war made logistics and supplies a challenge, but thus far, staff issues were the most time-consuming. The men seemed no more mature than the lads who would be arriving. *Lord, grant me the patience to lead without judgment. I don't know what these men have experienced. Are they single like me, or have they left wives behind? Or worse, have they lost their loved ones?*

Guilt pricked him. Once again, he'd let his ego get in the way, and he'd failed to see his colleagues through God's eyes, as fallible individuals in need of a Savior. "Forgive me, Lord. My temper has always been my nemesis. You must tire of me making the same mistakes over and over." He should have led by example and worked with the men to distribute the textbooks. Instead, he'd dictated the task, then hid out in his office. He barked a laugh. Mayhap the men would band together in their dislike of him.

"No time like the present to make amends." He ran his finger around his collar, then rolled down his sleeves and donned his suit coat. Would the men be horrified if he implemented a more casual dress code? Would that bond the students or create chaos with its laxness? Smoothing his tie, he strode across the room and yanked open the door.

At the end of the corridor, Stillwell and Martin pivoted and looked at him with wide eyes. Faces flushed, they resembled two children who'd been caught with their hands in the cookie jar. What were they up to? "Gentlemen, I'm glad to have found you. I wanted to apologize for not lending a hand."

"No problem, sir." Stillwell glanced at Martin. "We were out of line to complain. Won't happen again."

Gavin swallowed a sigh. "We're all trying to figure out how to make this work, so there will be fits and starts, but we'll muddle through, won't we?"

"Yes, sir." Martin rocked on his heels. "We've finished with the books. Anything else we can do?"

"No, enjoy the rest of the day. Tomorrow, too. Get settled in. We'll have a staff meeting on Thursday to discuss plans for moving forward. I'm going for a walk if either of you gents would like to join me."

Again, the pair exchanged a glance. What *were* they up to?

Stillwell shook his head. "Too warm for my blood, sir, but thank you for the offer."

"I respectfully decline as well." Martin gave him a wry smile. "Too much nature. I'm a city boy. I'll stick close to the house, if you don't mind."

Gavin chuckled. "You've got to get out there at some point, but I understand. I'm a Londoner myself. I haven't seen this much *nature* since university. See you at dinner."

The men's laugh that followed him down the hallway sounded forced, but relationships weren't formed overnight.

He pushed open the front door and stepped outside. A light breeze caressed his cheeks, and he raised his face toward the sun. He was glad for the solitude, but the men were missing out on Britain's beauty by remaining inside. Strolling along the lane that encircled the house, he ruminated about what he'd say at the meeting on Thursday to garner excitement from the teachers about their responsibilities.

Gravel crunched, and the hum of an engine sounded behind him. He turned as the horn blared. A black lorry bucked and swerved toward him. Pulse thundering, he leapt onto the grass. His feet tangled, and he fell to the ground in a heap, landing on his bad arm.

The vehicle stalled with a pop, and the door opened. A slender woman with jet-black hair, pulled into a ponytail, jumped out of the vehicle and rushed toward him. "Gracious, are you all right? I didn't mean to scare you or make you fall down." Her cornflower-blue eyes clouded with concern as she leaned over him. Her face pinked. "I'm a bit rusty at driving, I'm afraid."

"A bit? You almost killed me. You obviously have no business being behind the wheel." He looked past her at the lorry. "Who are you and why are you here? This is private property. You have no business being here."

Her eyes narrowed and darkened to sapphire. "There's no call to be nasty. I've apologized, and I was not driving fast enough to kill you. You're certainly one for dramatics, aren't you?" She put her hands on her hips. "And as for your declaration that I don't belong here, you're wrong. I'm Isobel Turvine, and I've been assigned to this estate by the Ministry of Agriculture."

"You're one of the land girls?" He cringed at the sarcasm in his tone. "I mean—"

"I know exactly what you mean, and if you're through insulting me, it appears you'll live, so I'll be on my way."

"I—"

"Save your breath." She turned on her heel and stomped to the lorry. She climbed inside, and seconds later, the engine roared to life. The vehicle lurched, then the woman gained control, and with gravel popping, the lorry shot past.

"Well, that went well, Emerson. Is there anyone you're not going to anger today?" Arm throbbing, He climbed to his feet and brushed dirt and grass from his suit. The earl had informed him about the WLA, yet he'd forgotten all about the women. Hopefully, that would be the last interaction he'd have with them. The woman's face floated into his head. What was her name? Isobel. Exotic. A bit like her with snapping blue eyes and shining black hair in a complexion not as pale as most women. Not as young as he'd thought a land girl would be. Near his age? No, but definitely not in her twenties. "Get a grip, old man. She's here to do a job, and so are you.

A Lesson in Love

Chapter Four

Isobel tugged her dark-green jumper down over her hips as she inspected herself in the mirror's reflection. Not her best color, but she wasn't here to win fashion awards. The tan breeches were more comfortable than they looked as were the matching socks. With a groan, she poked her feet into the sturdy brown shoes, then bent to tie the laces. Her muscles protested from the hours of unpacking seeds and other necessities. How bad would she hurt after working in the fields for twelve hours a day?

A knock sounded, and she turned.

"Is the student ready?" Tracey Gillam, one of the land girls, who had grown up farming, stood in the doorway, a bright smile on her face. She rubbed her palms together. "I can't wait to get my hands on this new John Deere. My family didn't have enough money for the likes of that."

Grabbing her wide-brimmed hat from the bed, Isobel walked toward the woman. "Then how did you plow?"

"With horses, silly. And sometimes by hand." With a giggle, Tracey shook her head. "You city girls are going to be the death of me."

Isobel's face warmed, and she shrugged. "Shows you how desperate the country is to hire us, isn't it?"

"I'm sorry. I didn't mean to poke fun." Tracey gave her a quick one-armed hug. "We all have to start somewhere, and I'm impressed you would apply for a job you don't know anything about. Takes guts."

"Thanks. Margery talked me into it. She was looking to get out of London, somewhere safer, you know? Anyway, the idea of producing food for the troops appealed to me. The boys are the real heroes marching off to war, and they deserve the best."

A shadow crossed Tracey's face. "That they do."

"You have family serving, don't you?"

"Yes, my brothers Terry and Tom. Barely out of secondary school. They should be at university, not carrying guns and shooting at other boys. What has this world come to?"

"Someone has to stop Hitler."

"I know. I just wish it didn't have to be my little brothers." Tracey shoved her hat onto her ginger curls. "Come on, we've got a tractor to tame."

"You know you're supposed to wear that think squarely on your head." Isobel yanked on the brim of her friend's hat. "As your leader, I'm going to ensure you pay strict attention to the rules."

Tracey snorted a laugh, then whipped off her hat and swatted Isobel. "Yeah, right. You're nothing but an old softie."

Isobel grinned. "Not quite, but I do find some of the rules ridiculous."

They walked down the hallway and out of the stone cottage. Her shoes crunched on the gravel path that led from the small house toward the barn and other outbuildings. A second path led to the manor home. The team wouldn't officially begin their work until Saturday after the rest of the workers came tomorrow.

Isobel had informed the women about her lack of knowledge, and the earl's insistence that she be in charge and act as liaison. Instead of being upset, they'd been relieved she would have to handle him. Tracey had quickly volunteered to show her the ropes, and the others assured her they had experience and would support her as well. With any luck, the remaining workers would be just as easygoing.

The sun crested the trees surrounding the property, and Isobel inhaled deeply. How long would it take her to get used to the smell of country air? It was surprisingly more fragrant than she anticipated. Gone were the sharp tang of coal and the gritty odor of chimney smoke, but there were distinctive smells carried in the breeze she couldn't define yet. Earthy, yes, but something else she couldn't pinpoint.

A few minutes later, they entered the barn where more odors assaulted her. Worse than being crammed in the Tube with half of London, during a Monday morning ride to work. Tracey hurried forward, then yanked the canvas cover from the green-and-yellow machine and squealed, "Isn't she a beauty?"

"She?"

"Of course, all of us gals are working together. She's another member of the team."

Isobel rolled her eyes. "Whatever you say. If you're so smitten, perhaps you should drive *her*."

"If I remember correctly, *someone* said everyone would learn all the jobs."

"That was before I met this monstrosity."

Tracey put her hands on her hips. "Is that any way to talk about Greta?"

"You've given her a name?" Isobel snickered. "You are something else, Tracey, but I like your style."

"Thanks." The woman looked pleased and beckoned Isobel closer. "Enough chatter. We'll go through this as many times as you need, but you're a smart one."

"I appreciate your confidence in me." Isobel trudged forward. The vehicle looked even bigger close-up, although the petroleum smell was familiar. London streets were full of the acrid odor of engines.

"This is a hand-start model, but if you follow the steps in the right order, she'll be purring in no time." Tracey pointed to a small tin can on top of the exhaust pipe. "The earl, or whoever delivered this baby, knows what he's doing. That will keep the mice out of the engine when the tractor isn't in use, so don't forget to put it back at the end of each day."

Isobel shuddered. A tip about keeping mice out of the engine? Was it too late to resign? Unfortunately, she wasn't a quitter.

Gavin swallowed a sigh as the five students he'd decided to take on a tour of the grounds poked and prodded each other and seemed to ignore everything he'd said thus far. He'd learned early on in his career that creating boundaries for pupils went a long way in keeping them out of trouble. With any luck, showing them around the property would make them less likely to strike off on their own to explore and potentially end up somewhere they shouldn't. Unlike his father, he could be firm without being overbearing or nasty.

Blinking, he shoved away the thought to focus on the boys. They'd shown marginal interest in the house, but by the time they tramped to the servant cottages turned land-army billet, their attention had waned. Now, they were headed to the barn.

Laughter floated across the breeze, and he pivoted toward the fields, the vibrant brown dirt contrasting with the surrounding pastures the workers hadn't gotten to yet. The two dozen women regularly worked from before dawn until well after the dinner hour, and their efforts had paid off. His back ached at the thought of turning all that soil. They'd gotten a late start by arriving in August, but despite the optimists who claimed the war would be over by Christmas, most people knew that wasn't the case. By preparing the land for next year, the group would have a head start on next season.

He squinted as his gaze bounced from one uniformed woman to the next, searching for the one who'd nearly run him down. Almost two weeks had passed since the incident, and he'd only caught sight of her periodically. Despite their identical garb, he'd know when he saw her. Her lithe form was neither extra tall nor short, but her graceful stride set her apart from the others. She held her head high, not in an arrogant manner, but confident. He imagined her blue eyes flashing with wit and intelligence. The broad-brimmed hat was always on her head, but he'd never forget the blue-black hair that poured down her back.

"Mr. Emerson, come see!"

Gavin's head whipped toward the voice. They'd approached the barn, and he'd been so immersed in the land girls—well, one particular land girl—he missed the fact that all but one of the lads had skipped ahead and ducked inside the building. On their own they could get into no end of trouble. He hurried through the open door and stopped short, taking in the scene.

Three of the boys pointed and guffawed at Harry who had climbed onto one of the cows and was digging his heels into her side. "Giddyup!" The poor animal was bellowing its discontent.

"Harry, get down this instant." Gavin rushed forward. "You'll injure the cow and could get hurt."

The fourteen-year-old scowled, but he slipped to the ground. "Aww, you're no fun, Mr. Emerson."

If Gavin didn't know better, he'd think the animal seemed relieved to be free of the prankster, thanking him with her eyes and a slight dip of her head. "The key to fun, Mr. Kemp, is responsibility. There are many ways to enjoy yourself, but endangering others and playing with something that doesn't belong to you, isn't one of them."

"I told you not to get on the beastie."

"There's no need to be an I-told-you-so, Mr. Corrigan." Gavin clapped his hands. "Now, as you can see, the barn is a fascinating place, but I'm not fully versed on its contents, so at some point I will have one of the land-army gals educate you. For the moment, I simply wanted you to see it and be told it is off-limits. Under no circumstances are you to come here. There are dangerous tools, but just as important is the fact that the women don't need you underfoot, messing with the animals, or fiddling with their equipment." He looked down his nose at each of the boys, one at a time. "Understood?"

"Yes, sir." With the exception of Harry, the boys spoke in unison. He shrugged and scuffed his shoe in the dirt floor. The young man had been a handful since he'd arrived four days ago. Orphaned after the Blitz, he'd been passed around to an uncle, then his grandparents, and finally a distant cousin, who'd apparently jumped at the chance to board him at school. No wonder the lad was difficult. Negative attention was better than no attention.

"Would you rather ride a horse, Harry?" Gavin tilted his head. "Admittedly, I know nothing about them, but I'll see if any of them might fancy a day with you lads."

Harry's eyes lit for a split second, then dimmed. Another shrug. "Don't matter none to me, but iff'n you want, I suppose that'd be fine."

Gavin squelched the desire to pump the air with his fist. The offer had appealed to the young man, although he was loathe to show his interest. Now, to follow through. Gavin would not be yet another adult letting him down.

Would the blue-eyed beauty be a help or a hindrance with his request?

A Lesson in Love

Chapter Five

As pink fingers pushed back the predawn darkness, Isobel strolled along the path that led to the barn. Movement caught her eye. Something was creeping among the collection of wooden crates piled near the building and headed away from the entrance. She stopped and squinted against the murky morning rays. A wild animal? Her pulse raced. She still struggled to be comfortable around the cows, their huge, widely space eyes that seemed to watch her every move, and their large lumbering bodies that could easily crush her against the wall. None of the girls seemed to mind that she didn't take a turn milking the cows, but sooner or later she needed to screw up her courage. As the women's leader, she needed to…lead.

She turned on the torch and swept the beam along the outside of the building. Whatever she saw couldn't be a wild animal. If it was, the creature would creep toward the entrance not away. And if it had been inside, the other animals would have raised a ruckus. Her heart rate slowed, and she continued her trek toward the barn. Seconds later, one of the boys emerged from behind the crates. He rose in full view of the light. His gaze rested on her, and a sardonic smile split his face before he took off at a run toward the main house.

What had he been up to? Nothing good, if his expression was anything to go by. She'd never catch him, but she needed to ensure he hadn't damaged anything inside the barn. Isobel broke into a jog, and her breath was loud in her ears as she covered the remaining distance to the building. She arrived at the doorway. Snuffling sounded from the horses in their stalls, and the half-dozen cows rolled their heads to her as one. The one closest to the entrance lowed, but more in greeting than distress. She raked her gaze over the walls of tools, but saw nothing out of place or missing.

The canvas covering the tractor was slightly off-kilter. Isobel rushed forward. Had the lad tampered with the machine? She yanked on the tarp, and it slid to the ground. The tin can was still in place over the exhaust pipe. She ran her hands along the flywheel, then fingered the choke as she checked the ignition switch and throttle. Nothing seemed out of place. Had the boy simply been curious or bored and done some exploring in the early morning hours? Should she report his presence in the barn? Mr. Emerson and the earl both indicated the lads had been instructed to stay out of the women's way, but perhaps the young man actually held an interest in farmwork. The school had been based in London, but maybe he was from one of the city's villages in the outskirts.

With a shrug, she shoved the canvas against the wall. No harm seemed to have been done, so she'd let his visit pass this time.

"Good morning."

Isobel whirled. She'd been so intent upon the tractor she'd failed to hear Tracey approach. "Good morning. Sleep well?"

"Always. Exhaustion will do that to a girl."

Giggling, Isobel nodded. "I must admit I don't have any trouble falling asleep either. I thought it was Ethel's turn to milk the cows this morning."

"Memorized the schedule, have you?"

"It helps to know where everyone is supposed to be." Isobel crossed her arms. "Is she all right? She doesn't usually shirk her duties."

"No fever, but she was feeling poorly last night, so we swapped to give her a couple extra hours of sleep."

"That was nice of you."

"I'd appreciate the same done for me if I was under the weather." Tracey's face pinked, and she shrugged. "Now, what are you doing in the barn at this time of day? We're not scheduled to get started for another hour."

"To be honest, I'm still trying to get my feet under me. I'm a teacher, not a manager, and I was raised with sidewalks and streets, not cows and tractors. The earl was adamant about my being in charge, but I feel like I'm barely one chapter ahead of the class."

"You're doing great. The girls respect you because you don't act like a know-it-all." Tracey grinned. "They're probably relieved not to be in charge themselves. Fortunately, the earl has seen to it that we have everything we need to do the job. Sharing the estate with the school is interesting."

"Speaking of the school, I saw one of the boys skulking about, and when he realized he'd been spotted, he sent me a rather mocking smile. I was surveying the barn when you arrived."

"That doesn't bode well." Tracey pursed her lips. "I'll help you."

"No, you need to get started on the milking."

"True, much longer, and they'll start complaining." Tracey turned on her heel and said in a singsong voice, "Coming, ladies."

Isobel snickered, then began a methodical search of the barn, shining the torch into the corners and crevices of the building. Nothing was out of place. She rubbed the back of her neck. The lad had done something. The expression he'd shot her said as much. What was she missing?

Turning back to the center of the barn, she studied the tractor, then strode toward the monstrous vehicle. She hadn't tried to start it. She turned on the choke, then the petrol gravity feed before ensuring the ignition switch was off and the gear was in neutral. So far, so good. She opened the throttle a tiny bit, then the petcock, and rotated the flywheel a couple of times to draw fuel into the cylinders. Opening the choke a bit more, she pulled on the ignition switch. "Here goes nothing." She gripped the flywheel and turned it to the left. The engine coughed, but didn't catch.

Isobel's mouth dried. "Don't panic, yet." She tightened her hold on the flywheel and turned it again. Another cough from the engine, then nothing. She didn't smell petrol. Had the lad siphoned the fuel? She walked to the other side of the tractor, then opened the tank cover. Her hand came away sticky. Sticky? She pointed the torch's beam at the opening. Small, white crystals clung to the metal. Her stomach clenched. "Tracey!"

Tracey poked her head around the back end of the cow. "What's wrong?"

"Come look." Isobel nibbled her lower lip.

"The little troublemaker's done something to the tractor, hasn't he?" She rose, patted the cow's rump, and hurried toward Isobel.

"Look at the tank."

Forehead etched in a deep V, Tracey snarled, "Wait until I get my hands on the brat. He should be flogged."

"It's sugar, isn't it?"

"Yes, and cleaning that mess out the system will take hours. That guttersnipe needs to suffer some sort of consequences."

Isobel huffed out a loud sigh. "We can't bother the earl with this. Not yet."

"He can't blame you." Tracey crossed her arms. "He's the one who allowed the urchins to take over the manor. You need to tell that looker of a headmaster. A bit old for me, but handsome for his age. He needs to discipline the lad, and I've got a few ideas as to how."

An image of Mr. Emerson's face floated into Isobel's mind. He was handsome no matter what his age, but she wouldn't debate the man's attributes. "Me, too. Every one of those boys needs to learn an appreciation for where their food comes from, and for the work we put in. I'm going to insist they be made to work in the fields."

"Or mucking out the stalls." Tracey snorted a laugh. "That will put a kink in their antics."

"Indeed." Isobel raised her chin. "I'll be back shortly."

"It's a bit early to be rousing the man from his bed."

"Perhaps being inconvenienced will help him understand the seriousness of the situation."

Tracey's face lit. "Too bad I've got to finish milking the cows. I'd really like to be there to watch."

"I'll be nice."

"I've seen your nice-but-firm schoolteacher thing. He doesn't have a chance."

Isobel winked at her friend. "No, but I'll let him think he does."

Chapter Six

Hunching deeper into his jacket, Gavin inhaled deeply as he strolled along the path that connected the series of gardens behind Kingsley Manor. The hedges were a bit ragged, but the beds were filled with a riot of color. What he knew about botany fit on the head of a pin, so he had no idea what the various flowers were, but the froth of pink, purple, yellow, and white blooms brought a smile to his face. Each of the gardens featured a focal point: a tiny pond in one, a trellis in another. Whimsical statuary was scattered throughout the gardens sparingly, but effectively.

One section included several topiary the earl himself kept trimmed. The man was an enigma: an interesting combination of Victorian manners and modern sensibilities. He loved to discuss history, and Gavin had talked him into guest lecturing to the students. The man had held the lads in rapt attention.

The sun still hid behind the trees, but its rays had pushed back the darkness, yet the night's chill remained. Initially, he'd taken to walking around the grounds each morning before breakfast to escape the constant interruptions by staff with problems they could easily handle themselves, but he'd come to enjoy the solitude. Just what he needed when planning his day.

Intrigued by the animals and what it took to care for them, he was tempted to wander toward the barn and other outbuildings, but he adhered to his rule of giving the women space. He expected the lads to remain out of the way, so he must do the same. In the distance, the rooster crowed, and Gavin chuckled. The bird was the biggest he'd ever seen, and its constant *cockle-doodle-do* throughout the day put to rest the myth that roosters only crowed at dawn.

A soft breeze laced with a mixture of soil, trees, and manure tugged at his hat. He'd grown used to the earthy odors different than the smell of London's coal and exhaust, but just as pervasive. The wind shifted, and the flowers' fragrance wafted toward him. He spied a wooden bench, rustic yet appearing new. Anything wrought-iron had been collected for the war effort, so the earl had apparently seen fit to replace the former seating. How long after the conflict would it take to bring back England's former glory?

He lowered himself onto the bench with a grunt and watched the mist dance and sway over the small pond, little more than a puddle. Ah, silence. He'd be subjected to the chatter and chaos of the boys soon enough.

"Mr. Emerson!"

Gavin jerked up his head and turned toward the voice. His eyes widened as Miss Turvine strode toward him, a deep scowl on her face. She wore her regulation Land Army uniform of tan knickers and dark-green jumper, but somehow managed to look stylish and sleek rather than frumpy. The broad-brimmed hat was pushed back on her head. Her eyes flashed blue flames.

His stomach hollowed, and he leapt to his feet. "What is it? What's happened?"

"The tractor has been tampered with, and one of your boys is the culprit."

"That's quite an accusation." He crossed his arms to refrain from shaking his finger at her. "Have you any proof?"

Hands on her hips, she tapped her foot. "Taking their side already?"

"Accusing them without cause already?" He heard the venom in his voice, but didn't back down. "The students are still abed. What makes you think one of them has been to the barn?"

"I've seen him. He was skulking away from the barn as I approached. When I caught him in the beam of my torch, he gave me a look that told me all I needed to know."

"A regular Hercule Poirot, are you?" Gavin bit back a sigh and motioned to the bench. "Look, this doesn't have to get adversarial. Why don't you have a seat while we sort this out?"

"I'd rather stand."

"Suit yourself." He stuffed his hands into his pockets. "I am concerned that one of the boys was out and about near the barn, but this isn't a prison. He may simply have been exploring."

"Even if that were true, we agreed the boys would give wide berth to the working area of the estate." She wrapped her arms around her middle. The anger had left her voice. "There are tools and machinery that can hurt them. Livestock, too. Or they could inadvertently harm the animals. You need to ensure they stay away from the barn and leave our equipment alone."

"And you need to stop making assumptions about the lads. I submit that just because you saw one of the students near the barn, and he *looked* guilty doesn't *make* him guilty. Perhaps a conversation with your girls is in order. Let them know they are here to work."

Her eyes narrowed. "You think one of my girls did this? What would prompt them to damage the tractor? For the pittance we're paid, it makes no sense that they'd hinder their ability to do the job."

"What if there is someone who doesn't want the work done, and, um, paid one of your girls to stop production?"

She gaped at him for a long second, then broke into loud laughter.

Gavin frowned as he watched her try to control her mirth. "I don't understand your reaction. It's a possible scenario."

"You have been reading Agatha Christie. She might come up with something like this, although in the end, one of us would be poisoned."

"I'm serious. What if one of the girls is a collaborator, or worse, a spy, someone hired to commit sabotage?"

"What if it's one of your teachers who is the fifth columnist or secret agent?" Isobel waved her hand in a dismissive gesture. "In all seriousness, I might believe your theory if I hadn't seen one of the boys near the barn, and if he hadn't given me a look that said he'd done some sort of mischief, and he was unconcerned about being caught. I've been a teacher for twelve years. I know when a student is up to something." She leveled her gaze at him. "And so do you. I understand why you'd rather not believe me, but at least remind the boys to limit their exploring to the house and nearby grounds and stay away from the barn and fields. Please."

"Fair enough." Gavin tugged at his collar. He hadn't expected their first extensive conversation to be a lecture from her. And she debated him point for point, confirming his estimation of the woman. She was no shrinking violet. The earl was right to put her in charge of the land girls. They would do the job, or she'd know why not. Dare he ask her about repairs to the tractor? He licked his lips. "Um, no matter who caused the problem, how are you going to get it fixed?"

Her slender shoulder lifted in a delicate shrug. "We'll take care of it ourselves. Unlike me, quite a few of the girls have farming experience and know their way around the machinery. In fact, Tracey is the one who taught me how to tackle the tractor. It's a hand-start model. You don't just turn a key or push a button. One of them should know how to repair it. I suspect we'll have to flush the system, but I don't know what that entails." She climbed to her feet. "And I must get to it."

"Wait. I, um, have an idea for later." Gavin tilted his head. "Don't answer until you've heard me out. What would you think about the lads helping you? They need to learn the sciences, and what better way then hands-on? Sort of a lab session after classroom time? They'd be closely supervised."

"No, I'm sorry. I know you're extending an olive branch, and the idea would be a good one in different circumstances, but we have production quotas, and the boys might hinder that." Isobel motioned toward the barn. "I need to get back. This has already taken longer than anticipated. See you round." Spine straight and arms swinging, Isobel strode along the garden path, then cut across the lawn.

"Well, Emerson, that was a debacle." Gavin took off his hat and slapped it against his thigh as he watched her. "Why couldn't you agree that the boy was probably the culprit? It's just the sort of prank you might have pulled as a student. Pride, old man, pure and simple."

"Arguing with yourself?"

Gavin whirled.

Alastair stood a few feet away, a broad grin on his face. "Already losing your mind?"

"Hardly. We've got a problem, and I'm not quite sure how to solve it."

"Might it have something to do with the attractive Miss Turvine disappearing over the hill?"

"Yes, but not in the way you're thinking." Gavin clamped his hat on his head. So maybe he had two problems associated with the attractive schoolteacher turned land girl, but he certainly wouldn't discuss it with Alastair even if the man was his best friend.

Chapter Seven

Perspiration trickled down the sides of Isobel's face, and she blew an errant strand of hair out of her eyes as she struggled to carry the sack of chicken feed from the lorry to the barn. The recalcitrant lock swung back across her face, and she snarled. Her shoulders and lower back throbbed, and her arms trembled with the heavy load. For the umpteenth time, she questioned her decision to join the Land Army.

She was ten to fifteen years older than most of the other women who sprang from their beds each morning, eager to tackle the day's tasks. They didn't groan or shuffle from the shared bathroom to the dormitory-style room in the evenings. Nor did they slump over their meals, exhausted and aching. They chattered and laughed as if they were at a dinner party.

The hens clustered around her as if they knew what she carried. "Go 'way, ladies. You've been fed." She scowled and dropped her burden on top of the other bags she'd already toted into the barn. Massaging the muscles in her upper arms, she moaned, then scolded herself. "Only one more bag, Turvine. Quit your groaning."

With a sigh, she stomped out of the barn to the lorry and tugged at the last bag. The string enclosure unraveled, and feed poured into the bed of the vehicle. Growling, Isobel wrapped the edges of the sack together to stop the flow. Now what? She couldn't lift the burden with one hand while preventing more spillage with the other.

Isobel twisted her neck to survey the fields. Thus far, the girls had converted nearly ten acres of meadow to fields, a fraction of the earl's immense property. The tractor had been used to first clear the land, then a second pass was made to prepare the soil for planting. She watched as they bent over the trenches, poked seed-potato segments into the ground, then shoved dirt over the chunk. Tracey had told her that, planted correctly, each acre could produce up to thirty thousand pounds of the vegetable. Isobel couldn't fathom that amount of food or what it was going to take to harvest it.

What she did know was that it would require them to work together which had thus far been the biggest challenge, other than her aching body. Two of the women didn't get along, and their bickering had divided the group, with some of the girls taking sides. Her efforts of mediation had proved fruitless. Even now from this distance, she could see their stiff body language. She had no doubt they had exchanged barbs and were now stewing over the conversation, if one could call it that.

With a sigh, she rolled her eyes, then put two fingers to her lips and whistled, a piercing sound that caused the women to raise their heads toward her. She cupped one hand around her mouth and shouted, "Tracey!" If still alive, her mother would be appalled, but then she wouldn't have understood Isobel's desire to join the Land Army. Ladies didn't shout or whistle or work farms.

Isobel shrugged. She'd disappointed her mother her entire life. Maybe it was a blessing Mum and Dad had been killed in the car accident on the way home from Isobel's graduation from teachers' college. She watched as Tracey jogged toward her, then motioned to the mess in the back of the lorry.

Her friend glanced down and snickered. "I thought I was the clumsy one. Thank you for not trying to do this yourself."

"Are you going to help or just make fun of me?"

"No need to get petulant." Tracey squeezed her shoulder. "You sound like Martha and Claire. All right, you keep a grip on the top, and I'll slide the sack toward us, then cradle it. Ready?"

"Yes."

"On three. One. Two. Three!"

Grunting, Tracey pulled the bag toward them, then wrapped her arms around it and lifted it from the lorry. Sack between them, they penguin-walked into the barn, then Tracey counted again, and they lowered their burden to the ground. "We'll sweep the spilled seed out of the lorry, and let the chickens clean it up for us. A little extra breakfast won't hurt them."

Isobel giggled, then leaned against the wall. "Thanks. I feel like such a dunce. How can I lead when I make silly mistakes?"

"You don't have to be perfect."

"No chance of that." Isobel swiped her hair out of her eyes with the back of her hand. "Are Martha and Claire squabbling again?"

"Martha claims Claire isn't giving her all for King and country."

Isobel's eyes widened. "A bit extreme, don't you think?"

"That's what Claire said." Tracey shrugged. "You know Martha says things like that to get a rise out of her. And it worked. If Claire would realize that and not let them wind her up…"

"I don't know what to do with those two. I'm a teacher, not a manager."

Tracey nudged her shoulder. "You are a manager, whether or not you like it. They're acting like your primary school kids, so treat them accordingly."

"You think?"

"Absolutely, and when they complain you're treating them like children, you can assure them you'll stop when their childish behavior stops."

"It's an idea." Isobel grabbed the broom and headed out of the barn, Tracey on her heels like an eager puppy. "Remind me why I took this job again?"

Tracey laughed. "To do *your* part for king and country."

"Right, and I'm not a quitter, although sometimes I wish I were." Isobel climbed into the lorry and began to sweep the feed out of the bed. Squawking, the chickens rushed toward the vehicle. She laughed as they jostled each other in their excitement. Tension slid from her shoulders. One task at a time. She looked toward the house as the front door opened, and Gavin stepped outside. At some point he'd stopped being Mr. Emerson in her mind, and she'd explore that little fact later. Much later.

Tracey slapped Isobel's leg. "Fancy a walk around the lawn?"

"Hardly. We've work to do. I've wasted enough time, and from the sound of it, I need to head to the fields and referee. Besides, at his age he's probably married, and the wife is staying with family or doing her bit somewhere."

"Nope." With a smug smile, Tracey shook her head. "I asked around. He's single. Never married and has no special lady in his life."

Isobel narrowed her eyes. "You've been busy, haven't you?"

"Someone had to do the reconnaissance." Tracey grinned and continued to look pleased with herself. "You were never going to do it."

"Well, thank you very much, but I'm not looking for a man, and I doubt he's looking for a woman. He would have found one by now."

"So, you agree he's handsome."

Isobel pressed her lips together. If she denied the allegation, she'd be lying. Best not to say anything. But from the look in Tracey's eyes, the girl knew Isobel's mind and would be like a dog with a bone about this particular topic.

Seated at the desk in the front of the classroom, Gavin graded papers while his students took a quiz. They'd been rambunctious at breakfast and barely concealed their fidgeting during his lecture, so in an effort to quell their restlessness, he'd announced a pop quiz. The groans could have been heard in London, but the test had the desired effect. He'd purposely created questions the lads could answer with minimal effort in an attempt to build their confidence about the topic, and it appeared to be working. Pencils scraped on paper, and a periodic murmur punctuated the silence as one of the boys realized he knew an answer.

Swallowing a smile, Gavin looked out the window. The day had dawned with glorious streaks of pink, purple, and orange. As the morning progressed, the sky turned cerulean-blue without a cloud to be seen. After three days of rain, the sunny day seemed especially bright. He understood the boys' behavior, but that didn't mean he had to allow it.

His gaze slid back to the boys. All ages, sizes, and maturity levels. Most were good lads, and the others weren't so much bad as responding to their feelings about being sent away from their families. The initial excitement about being on a farm with new sights, smells, and experiences had worn off. Chafing against the rules and inability to set off on their own like they might have in the city, some of the boys had gotten into mischief, the incident with the tractor only one example.

He disliked the idea of being stricter than he was already, but he had to come up with something to prevent them from injuring themselves or doing further damage on the estate. Alastair regularly took them tramping around the thousand-acre property to wear them out, but being boys, they had more energy than a cheetah on the hunt and more curiosity than the proverbial cat.

A whisper sounded from the back of the room, and he swung his vision over the bent heads, searching for the culprit. He studied each boy, but they all seemed intent on their work. He pursed his lips. He hadn't imagined the noise, but whoever had spoken was clever enough not to be caught.

Biting back a sigh, he scrubbed at his face with cold fingers and turned his attention back out the window. If he couldn't focus, why did he expect the lads to do so?

"Ouch!"

Jerking his head around, Gavin searched the classroom. Warren Sharp scowled at the student behind him while rubbing his calf. Peter Donovan, the alleged offender, had schooled his features into a bland expression of innocence. "Do we have a problem, gentlemen?"

"He kicked me, Mr. Emerson." Warren's gaze bounced back and forth between Peter and Gavin. "He wanted me to give him one of the answers, and when I didn't, he kicked me."

Gavin rose and strolled down the row toward the pair. Towering over them, he peered down his nose. "Any validity to his claim, Mr. Donovan?"

"He's lying." Peter shook his head, still the picture of innocence. "He doesn't like me because I'm smarter than him, and he's lying."

"I am not!" Face as red as a ripe tomato, Warren jumped up and swung at the boy who ducked. "You're nothing but a low-down, stinking—"

"Enough!" Gavin wrapped his arms around Warren, trapping his flailing limbs. "There will be no punching or name calling." He leveled his gaze at Peter who remained smug. "Or kicking. Now, I believe a change in venue is in order. For all of you." He released Warren who slumped beside him.

"I haven't finished my test, Mr. Emerson," one of the lads said from behind him.

"I haven't finished my test, Mr. Emerson." The second voice was falsetto and mocking.

Laughter spread throughout the classroom, and Gavin tamped down his irritation. If he lost his temper, he was no better than his students…or his father. The boys needed to see their worth despite their behavior. He'd treat the boys with a firm hand, but with an attitude of caring. He clapped his hands, and the frivolity stopped. "Pass your tests to the front. The results will determine whether or not they will count toward your final grade."

The buzz of conversation started, and Gavin clapped again. "I'm still talking, gentlemen. These are difficult times. I'd hazard a guess than none of you want to be living at school." He shot them a grin. "Your worst nightmare, I'd say. But we must make the best of the situation. How we respond to adversity proves our mettle, does it not?" As he spoke, he rested his eyes on the boys one by one. "I believe you have it within you to do the right thing. I believe you are up to the task, each and every one of you. But I also believe we've done you a disservice by not requiring you to contribute to your keep. When I was a lad and part of a family, I had chores that were required of me—"

A groan rose, and he stared them down, cutting off the noise. "I'll assume you don't want to hear about my childhood, that you're not expressing your displeasure at the prospect of contributing to your stay here." He glanced at the clock above the door. "It's nine thirty-two. You have thirteen minutes to go to your rooms, change into attire appropriate for outside work, and return here."

"Work?"

"But, Mr. Emerson…"

Complaints and more groans that he let continue for a full minute before saying, "Twelve minutes."

The boys yelped, and chairs scraped as they leapt to their feet, then scrambled for the door.

"Steady on, lads. No running in the hallways or disturbing the other classes." As the students departed, and their footsteps faded, Gavin rubbed the back of his neck. How to convince Miss Turvine of his plan? He should probably take reinforcements, but showing up with the boys in tow would have to do. Hopefully, she'd reprimand him in private.

A Lesson in Love

Chapter Eight

Clouds scudded across the sky, playing hide-and-seek with the sun as Isobel bent and poked another potato chunk into the soil. The odor of manure mingled with the earthy smell of dirt. Snippets of conversation swirled around her as the girls talked among themselves while they worked. The breeze shifted, and she could hear Ethel singing, her clear contralto voice belting out "Chattanooga Choo Choo," a song by the American Glenn Miller, recorded the previous year. During the day, she typically sang peppy numbers, while in the evening she regaled them with love songs. Her repertoire seemed endless.

Isobel snickered. At least the woman could carry a tune. A couple of the girls who occasionally joined her sounded like fighting cats, but Ethel graciously acted as if nothing was wrong. In fact, she usually encouraged them to sing. Fortunately, today the pair was more interested in chatting.

The day was cool, but perspiration adhered Isobel's blouse to her back as she moved forward along the trench. Grab a potato wedge from the basket. Poke the chunk into the dirt. Scoop soil on top. Tamp it down. Grab. Poke. Scoop. Tamp. Repeat.

She'd gotten adept at the task, and she flicked a glance to the girls on each side. Isobel grinned at the progress she'd made. She was six feet ahead of almost all the others. Not that it was a competition, but she needed to prove to them as well as herself she was fit for the job despite her age.

Laughter floated from the direction of the house, and she raised her head. Gavin and about a dozen boys were crossing the lawn and walking toward the fields. Her pulse tripped as she struggled to stand. How disheveled did she appear? Hopefully, there were no smudges on her face. She brushed dirt from her hands, then tugged her blouse into place. The brim of her hat only partially blocked the sun, and she squinted at the boys who followed their teacher like ducklings after their mother.

Normally rambunctious, the lads marched in two lines and managed to refrain from pushing and shoving or other antics. What had he said to ensure their good behavior? Had he threatened them or promised a treat? She knew nothing of his teaching style. Had he developed camaraderie with his students, or did they fear him? She studied his face. Tracey was right in her assessment. No matter his age, Gavin Emerson was a fine-looking man. He wasn't overly tall, but he bore himself with assurance. Dark hair glinted in the sun, and the white at his temples lent him an air of distinguished gentleman. Gray eyes snapped with intelligence that probably missed nothing. Did the fine lines around his eyes speak of a sense of humor?

As he approached, he raised one hand in greeting. He wore denim pants and a blue shirt with the cuffs rolled to his elbows, exposing his arms. Not overly muscled, but manly, nonetheless.

Isobel's mouth dried as she straightened, and she licked her lips. The bucket and ladle were too far away to take a swig of water. *Focus!* She pinned on a smile and stepped over the trenches to meet him at the edge of the field. He obviously had a plan for the boys to be outside. Was he there to ask permission? It was hardly hers to grant, but after the tractor incident, he and the lads had maintained a wide berth. Perhaps he wasn't as arrogant or difficult as she'd imagined.

"Miss Turvine, please forgive the intrusion." Gavin dipped his head, then motioned to the boys. "We're feeling a bit cooped up today and are looking for an opportunity to help earn our keep. We don't want to impede progress, but is there some task you might assign to us that doesn't require your keen oversight?"

She smiled at his use of "we" and "our" and his question. She'd turned down his first request, but perhaps she'd been hasty. She doubted the boys had suggested chores as a way to beat their cabin fever. How badly had they behaved? "I'm happy to have such strapping lads lend a hand here with the planting."

Most of the boys straightened and raised their chins, their expressions changing from amusement to pride. The rest looked at her with suspicion.

"Excellent." Gavin rubbed his hands together and sent her a conspiratorial grin as he winked. "We await your instructions."

Her breath caught. The man had winked at her. How audacious. She should be offended, but instead her pulse thrummed. "Yes, well, um, what we're doing here is planting potatoes which are an innocuous-looking vegetable but actually quite nutritious, with lots of potassium and vitamin C. Other things, too, but most important is how delicious they are. My favorite way to eat them is chips." She let her gaze bounce on each of the boys. "Don't you agree?"

They all grinned and nodded.

"Let's get cracking, shall we? We can't have them if we don't plant them." She reached into the basket and pulled out a potato chunk, the motioned toward the trenches. "You're going to take one of these and tuck it into the ground cut-side down, then push the dirt on top." She pointed to a dimple on the vegetable's skin. "This is the eye, and it faces up so the shoots can push through the soil and reach the sun. Plant them about twenty-five to thirty centimeters apart." She held up her hands to show the distance. "This is not a competition as to how fast you can plant, but rather how well you can do the job. Are you gentlemen up to the task?"

Cheering, the boys surged forward to look inside the potatoes.

Isobel chuckled. "We have to retrieve more baskets and potatoes. Who would like to help?"

All the students' hands went up, and she exchanged a glance with Gavin. Her cheeks heated. Admiration and something else she couldn't pinpoint was evident in his eyes. Her gaze slid back to the boys, and she motioned toward the barn. "Apparently, we're all going." She took a deep breath, then dared to send Gavin a ~~saucy~~ cheeky smile. "And you, sir, will remain here and get started on this basket."

Eyes twinkling, he straightened, then clicked his heels together and saluted. "Yes, ma'am."

She pivoted and shepherded the boys toward the barn. What had she gotten herself into?

Gavin blocked his eyes against the sun's glare as Miss Turvine strolled across the field, the boys close on her heels. He couldn't hear her words, but her animated face and the movement of her hands as she talked told him she was passionate about whatever she was saying. The lads seemed to be hanging on her every word. A frisson of envy slithered through him, and he shook his head. "Get a grip, old man."

Shaking his head, he picked up the basket with a grunt. He raised his head as Isobel and the boys disappeared into the barn. The load was heavier than it appeared, yet she'd hefted it as if it weighed little more than a Christmas turkey. The lovely Miss Turvine, no, Isobel—the formality was gone—was an enigma. She'd been surprised at his wink, but she'd responded in kind. Of average height yet slender, she seemed to be managing the work as well as any farmwife. He'd seen her on the tractor, opening and closing the huge gates that led to the pastures, and now, planting acres of spuds. She probably helped with milking and other chores. Her accent said she was London bred, but she'd taken to the work as if born to it.

"An enigma, to be sure." Gavin set the basket within reach, and with awkward motions grabbed a potato, then bent over the trench and dropped the chunk. It fell eye-side down, and he huffed out a breath. He rolled the piece, then shoved dirt on top. "At this rate, the troops will starve to death." He repeated the motions, this time without fumbling, and grinned. He wasn't adept yet, but perhaps there was hope.

Voices and laughter floated toward him, and he looked up. Two of the boys were pushing a cart filled with baskets. The others skipped alongside Isobel, chattering among themselves as if they were headed to a playground rather than a field for planting. She had them in the palm of her hand.

Moments later, they arrived at the edge of the field, and the lads distributed the baskets among themselves. Isobel patted Harry's shoulder, and he beamed at her. Gavin gaped at the boy, then chuckled. He wasn't the only male smitten with the young woman.

"All right, men. Pick a row and get started. I or one of the other gals will be by to check your initial efforts." She pressed her gloved hands against her chest. "We are grateful for your help. As you know, many hands make light work."

Reminiscent of puppies, the boys ran toward the rows.

"Mind the trenches, lads," Isobel shouted, and they halted, then picked their way across the walnut-colored soil. "Much better. Thank you." She watched them for a moment, then gestured to a nearby Land Girl. "Can you check their progress in a bit?"

The girl nodded, then went back to planting her row with a steady rhythm.

Gavin shook his head. In seconds she'd done triple his efforts. Would he and the lads be a help or hindrance? "Iso—Miss Turvine, it's kind of you to take us on. Please tell me we won't be an impediment."

She removed her broad-brimmed hat and fanned her face. Strands of charcoal-colored hair wafted in the breeze. "They'll get the hang of it, as will you. We weren't nearly as efficient with the first field. And frankly, anything you all plant is that many fewer for us. We welcome the assistance." She plunked her hat on her head, which shadowed her eyes. "The short time I had with you in the barn, explaining the process, was a joy. To be honest, I miss teaching." She shrugged and carried her basket to the next row. "My country needs me, so…"

Gavin caught his teeth in his lower lip before he could blurt out an offer to let her into the classrooms. The men would mutiny. A boys' school called for male teachers. Didn't it? That was certainly tradition, but if he'd learned one thing as a result of the war, traditions were becoming a thing of the past, especially where the female of the species was concerned. They were in the factories, the fields, and the armed forces, albeit not carrying weapons. He'd also heard rumors women were being used as spies. Unimaginable, but he wouldn't be surprised. Churchill seemed a clever fox, and if he thought women could get the job done, he'd use them.

"Mr. Emerson, are you having a problem?"

Face heating, Gavin glanced at Isobel who stood with her hands on her hips, head cocked. "Oh, um, no, just woolgathering."

She grinned at him. "You've got to get cracking at some point. We can't let the lads get ahead of us."

"Or we could let them feel good about themselves by beating us."

Laughter burst from her lips, bringing to mind the tinkling of silver bells. Her eyes sparkled.

His chest swelled. She thought he was amusing.

She shook her finger at him, her expression on of mock sternness. "True, however, we must also consider leading by example."

"Yes, ma'am. You're quite right." He bent to his work but could feel her stare. What did she think of him? Yes, he'd made her laugh, but a little frivolity always made chores easier.

They worked in silence for a while; he lost time as the sun crept higher. His hands ached, and needles of pain stabbed his back and the crumpled scar on his arm, but far be it for him to give up before the boys or the women, especially the women. Sweat trickled down the sides of his face, and he swiped at the moisture with the back of his hand. He reached into the basket and hit the bottom. Peeking over the rim, he exhaled. Empty, which meant he had a reprieve. He straightened and massaged his lower back with a grimace. At least he'd sleep well.

"Not bad, Mr. Emerson, not bad at all." Isobel's voice came from behind him, and he turned. On her knees, she smiled at him.

He chuckled, then beat his chest with both hands and emitted a Tarzan-like yell Johnny Weissmuller would be proud of. "Not bad for an old man, you mean."

Isobel climbed to her feet. "Old man, hardly. You can't be much older than me."

"Sweet of you to say, but I'll hit forty-six on my next birthday."

"I would not have guessed. You're mighty fit." Then as if she realized what she said, her cheeks blazed, and she ducked her head. "I mean—"

"I'll take the compliment, thank you very much." Perhaps he wasn't as washed up as he'd believed.

A Lesson in Love

Chapter Nine

Gavin worked in silence next to Isobel, occasionally raising his head to check on the boys. Whether from true interest in planting or the opportunity to spend a portion of their day with pretty girls, the boys seemed to have settled down and focused on their task. He slid his gaze toward Isobel who was intent on her own row. A lock of hair had escaped from her braid and dangled beside her pink cheek, flushed from the heat of the day. Sunlight caused the raven-black strand to shimmer and appear almost blue.

She turned her head. "Do you need something, Mr. Emerson?"

His gut tightened. He'd been caught staring. "Um, no, just, uh, seeing how far you'd progressed; you know, in comparison to me."

A corner of her mouth turned up, and her blue eyes sparkled like topaz. "I didn't realize we were in competition."

"Hard habit to break."

"Perhaps I should take you on in chess to see just how deep that competitive streak runs."

His eyebrows shot up. "You play chess?"

"You don't think it possible for a woman to play?" A frown darkened her face. "How—"

"No, but other than my mother, I've not met a woman who does."

"Your mother?" Isobel sat back on her haunches, her face a delightful shade of red. "Please accept my apology."

Gavin waved a dirt-encrusted hand and grinned. "No need. We both seem ready to jump to conclusions about each other. I'll try to refrain if you will."

"Fair enough." She swiveled her neck and surveyed the field, then brought her attention back to him. "You've done well with the students. I wouldn't have thought they'd be so…"

"Helpful?" He chuckled. "Neither did I. Honestly, they were running roughshod over me, and I decided wearing them out with a little physical labor might also give them a greater appreciation for where their food came from."

She met his smile with one of her own. "Clever."

His pulse stuttered. How did she manage to look so lovely in the unflattering uniform with a smudge of dirt on her face? He cleared his throat. "You'd have done the same or would have been able to control them better."

"Doubtful. I haven't been able to get two of the girls to quit bickering." She wrinkled her nose. "They're no better than my primary school students."

"I've got a pair like that. I still can't decide if I can trust them."

"Mr. Emerson!"

Stillwell's voice floated across the expanse as he hurried toward them.

"And here comes one of them now."

Gavin climbed to his feet. His scar tissue ached, but he refrained from massaging the offending area. Prideful perhaps, but sometimes pride was all he had left. "Stillwell, what gives?"

"It's Harry, sir. He's at it again."

"How is that possible?" Gavin motioned to the young man several meters away. "He's been with me for the last two hours."

"Oh, well, um, it was Mr. Martin who fingered the lad as the culprit."

"Perhaps Mr. Martin should do a bit more investigating, wouldn't you say?" Gavin leveled his gaze at the man. "What is Mr. Kemp supposed to have done?"

"Trapped the rooster in one of the women's cottages."

"The rooster?" Gavin's breath exploded, and he yanked off his hat. "What… How… That bird…" He turned to Isobel who had also risen. "I need to sort this out. The boys—"

"Will be fine with us."

"Aren't you angry? Who knows what that bird has done?"

"You appear to be upset enough for both of us, and as you said, this requires more investigation. Your students may not have anything to do with this. One of my gals could have left a window open. So, let's not exacerbate the situation by jumping to conclusions, shall we?" She tilted her head as she looked at Stillwell. By this time, the WLA gal from the next row had stood up and joined them.

Gavin swallowed a smile as the man's expression changed to embarrassment. "Quite right." He brushed dirt from his hands. "Are you sure about the lads staying with you? I can pawn them off on one of the other teachers."

"Absolutely not. We'll be sure to wear them out for you, but I'll send Margery along to ascertain the extent of the damage in the cottage."

"Of course. We'll be there straight away, Stillwater."

The teacher gave them all a curt nod, wheeled around, and headed toward the cottages.

Gavin cupped his hands around his mouth. "Lads, I must take of something in the school. Please mind Miss Turvine. I'll return as soon as I can." He received a handful of nods, but most of the students either couldn't hear him or chose to ignore his command. Careful to avoid slogging through the trenches, he picked his way across the rows. Isobel's voice wafted toward him.

"All right, gentlemen. Mr. Emerson apparently thinks you'll misbehave after he leaves, but I know you can prove him wrong. You're doing a brilliant job. Let's keep up the good work."

Gavin squelched the desire to turn and look at the boys' expressions, but he wouldn't risk letting her realize he'd heard her. Or had she meant for him to hear what she'd said? As they tromped toward the collection of stone cottages, he peeked at the woman beside him, then blinked as he discovered her staring at him, an inscrutable look on her face. "May I help you?"

"Just trying to figure you out." She motioned toward his clothing. "Didn't think you're someone to own the likes of that. You dress like a toff to teach the lads. So, which is the real you?"

"I assure you, Miss...?"

"Vincent. Margery Vincent."

"I assure you, Miss Vincent, I'm a teacher, nothing more, nothing less. We have standards about our attire, but I hardly wear the clothes a rich man could afford. Are you as judgmental about everyone you meet?"

The woman had the grace to blush. "Just don't want to see my friend get hurt."

"Your friend? Miss Turvine? We've barely interacted. You and she have nothing to fear." He glanced at Margery. "I appreciate your loyalty to her. Have you been friends long?"

"We met in high school. Both of us were in the crowds outside Westminster Abbey when Princess Anne got married."

Gavin tucked his hands into his pockets as he searched his memory for the year the only daughter of the Duke and Duchess of York married. Nineteen twenty-one? Twenty-two? That put Isobel and her friend at one side or the other of thirty-five. Ten years or more younger than him. Another reason she'd never be interested in him. He nibbled the inside of his cheek. A moot point since he was not in the market for a wife. But if he were—

"I thought it would be a problem to work for her since she's my best friend, but that's not been the case at all. Not that I actually work for her, but she is in charge. She's fair, not asking us to do anything she won't do. She's had it tough, but she hasn't let that make her bitter. No, sir. She knows others have had it worse. 'Course, other than being widowed, there's nothing harder than losing your folks. Even after a bomb killed our other friend, she didn't let herself get down. In fact, she was going to stay in London until I convinced her otherwise. I wasn't going to stay where the Jerries were trying to kill us."

Biting back a smile at the woman's rambling, Gavin nodded to let her know he was listening. How would Isobel feel about the woman sharing her personal story?

They arrived at the cottage where Stillwater stood next to the open door. Gavin motioned for Miss Vincent to precede him, then followed her inside. She stopped short. "Well, this is going to take more than a rag or two."

He looked over her shoulder and grimaced as he rolled up his sleeves. "And more than one person. I'll lend you a hand, then we'll figure out how the little terror got inside."

She stared at him for a long moment, then grinned. "Nope, not a toff. You'll do, Mr. Emerson, you'll do."

With a chuckle, he nudged her shoulder. "I'm happy to know I've passed muster."

Her face pinked, and she shrugged. "Didn't mean to offend you, sir. Isobel says my mouth is going to get me into hot water one of these days."

"No offense taken, and there's no reason for Miss Turvine to be privy to our conversation. I'll fetch the cleaning supplies, if you'll set things to rights." He turned on his heel and trotted out of the cottage, then frowned. Stillwater had disappeared. Gavin would deal with the man later. What else would he learn about Isobel from her voluble friend?

A Lesson in Love

Chapter Ten

"Come on, gorgeous. The rest of us need a turn at the mirror." Margery's voice was muffled from behind the door. "I'm going to faint if I don't eat soon."

Isobel chuckled, then finished applying her lipstick before opening the door. "I'm fairly certain you're not going to faint, but point taken. I want to look my best for the boys. They've worked hard to prepare dinner for us."

"Yeah, I'm sure it's the lads you're aiming to impress." Margery smirked as she slipped into the bathroom. "You look fabulous, by the way. He'll be sure to notice you."

"I can't imagine who you mean."

"Your pink cheeks say differently." The door slammed, but her friend's laughter could still be heard.

"Not everyone is husband-hunting," Isobel muttered as she stalked into the room she shared with Margery, Tracey, and three other girls. She dropped onto her bed and snatched up the Agatha Christie mystery she'd been reading, which brought to mind the argument she'd had with Gavin about the tractor. With a huff, she flung the book, and it hit the floor with a thump. Was Margery correct that Isobel wanted to impress the man?

Sighing, she got up and retrieved the book. Nonsense. He was nice enough, but her life was fine like it was. She could do what she wanted when she wanted without asking some man for permission. Admittedly, she was making assumptions about Gavin, but he'd been overbearing on more than one occasion. The tractor wasn't the only incident. Sure, they'd come to a truce, and he seemed to be making an effort to be more amenable, but a leopard never changed its spots or a man his ways.

Footsteps sounded in the hallway, and Margery appeared in the doorway, a cheeky smile on her face. "I'm finally ready, Cinderella. If someone hadn't hogged the bathroom—"

"I beg your forgiveness." Isobel slid her keys into the pocket of her skirt as she stuck out her tongue.

Margery guffawed, flipped her long, blonde tresses over her shoulder, then headed down the hall. "Last one there is a rotten egg."

Isobel grinned as she hurried to catch up with her friend. Outside, she watched her friend race toward the brick-and-stone manor, her hair streaming behind her. Breaking into a run, Isobel sprinted across the lush green lawn. She couldn't imagine life without the girl. At times exasperating and exhausting, she was the Rock of Gibraltar, never wavering in her support during the awful days, weeks, and months following the accident that took Isobel's parents. Margery's giggle floated toward her, and the tightness at the memory of her mum and dad eased in Isobel's chest.

Arriving at the door a few seconds behind Margery, Isobel took a deep breath. So much for the care she'd put into pinning up her hair. She tugged out the pins holding the loose chignon, then finger-combed her thick locks. She swatted her friend. "You're incorrigible."

"Yes, but you love me anyway." Margery checked her wristwatch, then swung open the door. "At least we're only fashionably late."

Isobel wouldn't give her the satisfaction of an apology as she followed her into the dining room. She halted in the doorway, and her jaw dropped. The earl had apparently given the boys access to his cabinets. Each table was covered in a pristine white cloth with a crystal candlestick gracing the center. Silverware gleamed in the flickering light. If she wasn't mistaken, the china was Royal Doulton. Savory fragrances rose from steaming bowls and platters. Pitchers clinked against crystal goblets as the girls chattered among themselves.

Hair slicked down and dressed in white shirts and dark pants, the lads were flanked by several teachers near the door to the kitchen. Of its own volition, her gaze sought the face of the headmaster, and she gulped. He was staring at her, and she stifled the desire to turn tail and return to the cottage.

Margery jabbed her with an elbow. "Let's find a table, Cinderella."

"Stop calling me that." Hearing the sharpness in her voice, Isobel huffed a sigh. "Sorry. Guess I'm a bit more tired than I thought."

"As you should be. The last field is planted, and we've you to thank for that."

They threaded their way to the table where Tracey pointed to a pair of vacant chairs. Several of the girls called out greetings as they passed, and Isobel tried to acknowledge each one before sitting down.

"That dreamy headmaster already said grace so you can dig in." Ethel waved her fork toward the platter of succulent-looking ham. "And there's more where that came from."

Martha scowled as she jabbed at a carrot chunk. "I didn't know those poor boys had a preacher for headmaster, pushing his beliefs on to us by praying."

"You don't have to listen if you don't want," Claire piped up. "I, for one, think it's a nice touch."

"Of—"

"Ladies, please set aside your differences for the evening." Isobel speared the two of them with her best teacher-evil-eye. "Let's appreciate the effort the boys have made and enjoy our food. There's much to celebrate. You all worked hard today, and we finished the field ahead of schedule."

"Yes, miss." Claire ducked her head, but Martha continued to look mulish.

Isobel served herself from each of the items on the table, then began to eat. Salty flavor exploded in her mouth. Who knew a bunch of men and rambunctious boys could put together such a feast? Had the boys managed the meal on their own or received assistance from the cook? Whatever the case, she'd be sure to thank them when the meal was over. Letting the conversation swirl around her, she took another bite of ham and nearly moaned. If nothing else, having access to this quality of food rather than tinned meals was worth the aches and pains. Minutes passed as she tucked into her food, and the conversation ebbed and flowed around her.

Clapping sounded, and she turned to the front of the room. Gavin waved his arms, and the noise ceased. "Thank you for joining us for dinner, ladies. We hope you've enjoyed our attempts at cooking. If you're not too tired, the lads would like lead you in a game of charades." His gaze rested on her face with a questioning expression.

Should she mandate the women's participation?

"You're not required to play. After all, you've had a long day in the sun, so we'll start in…" Gavin pulled out his pocket watch and popped it open. "Fifteen minutes. That will give us time to clear the table and anyone who isn't interested, a chance to flee the room." He sent her a cheeky smile, then bent to listen to the boy next to him.

Isobel's cheeks heated. Was he speaking directly to her? Did he think she wanted to leave? Suddenly no longer tired, she couldn't wait to prove her fortitude against him. She looked at the other women. None of them made a move to leave, and Isobel's heart swelled. Even Martha and Claire, who didn't seem to like anything, remained in their seats, a look of eagerness on their faces. The evening took on a brighter shine.

"All right, lads. Time to clear the tables. Slow and steady, just like we instructed you." Gavin motioned for the boys to begin their task, then before he could change his mind, he threaded his way to Isobel's table. Her back was to him, her black hair shimmering under the chandelier. She must have been talking because her hands moved almost like a maestro conducting an orchestra. One of the women, what was her name…Mavis, Margaret, no, Margery, grinned at him, then waggled her eyebrows and said something. The group erupted with laughter, and Isobel's shoulders stiffened. Two of the ladies glanced in his direction as she turned around, her cheeks tinged with pink.

He hesitated, then pinned on a smile and stopped at the nearest table rather than continue toward Isobel's. "Good evening, ladies. I hope you enjoyed your meal."

Several of the women nodded and murmured their thanks.

To prevent further embarrassment for Isobel, he quashed the desire to let his gaze rest on her, telling her with his eyes how glad he was to see her. He moved to another group. "Thank you for being the lads' guinea pigs."

The sound of breaking glass filled the room, then a clatter of metal, followed by, "You pushed me!"

Gavin's head whipped up in time to see Harry shove Nigel. "I did not. Take it back."

"Look what you made me do." Nigel stumbled but managed to remain upright.

The boys were next to Isobel's table, and as Nigel took a swing at Harry, she reached out with lightning speed and grasped Nigel's arm. She said something Gavin couldn't hear, and the boy's shoulders slumped as he shook his head.

As Gavin threaded his way through the room, some of the women rose to get a better look at the altercation. "Pardon me, miss." He squeezed past a particularly large woman, then arrived as Harry and Nigel were shaking hands.

Isobel beamed at the boys as if they'd brokered an end to the war. "Well done, gentlemen. Now, remember what I told you."

"Yes, Miss Turvine," they chimed in unison, then bowed to the others at the table. As Harry bent to pick up the shards of soiled china, Nigel said, "We're sorry for causing a kerfluffle. It won't happen again." He then looked at Harry. "I'm going to get rags and a bucket. Will you be all right while I'm gone?"

"Yes, thank you for asking."

Gavin gaped at the boys whose conversation was reminiscent of two men having dinner at the club. He expected them to refer to each other as "old chap" at any moment. "It appears you have everything in hand, Miss Turvine."

Isobel shot him a satisfied smile as she rose. "Just a little misunderstanding. They're keyed up from all the excitement."

"If you say so, but they must learn that violence is rarely the answer."

"Yet, they are far from home without their families because of a war that has nothing to do with them. They promised to refrain from punching as a solution the next time their tempers flare, so let's give them the benefit of the doubt, shall we? If there is a second transgression, perhaps a stronger response will be necessary."

He narrowed his eyes and tamped down his irritation. "Are you telling me how to do my job, Miss Turvine? The lads are my responsibility, and I can't have them acting like a bunch of hooligans and knocking the seven bells out of each other." His voice was sharp in his ears.

One eyebrow lifted, and she crossed her arms. "A mere scuffle, but do what you think is best, Mr. Emerson. Far be it from me, a lowly former primary school teacher to instruct a mighty headmaster, but I have found a firm but loving manner goes further than a heavy hand."

Chastised, he fought the urge to duck his head. "Quite right, Miss Turvine. My apologies. Perhaps I let my pride get in the way. Again. Hopefully, I haven't ruined the evening, and you and your ladies will stay for charades."

"We wouldn't miss it for anything." She bestowed one of her dazzling smiles on him as if they hadn't just exchanged harsh words, then glanced at her tablemates. "Isn't that right?"

They nodded as one, and she turned back to him. "It's settled, and all is forgiven."

"You're most gracious." Before he could say anything else that might lodge his foot firmly into his mouth, he pivoted and headed toward the kitchen where he could oversee cleanup. He shouldered his way through the swinging door as Harry lifted a bucket from the sink.

The young man's cheeks bloomed red. "I'm sorry, Mr. Emerson. Nigel and I both are."

"It's over and done with, Mr. Kemp. No need to apologize again. I'm proud of you for taking responsibility for your actions. You've the makings of a fine man."

Harry straightened his spine. "Yes, sir. Thank you, sir. Best get to it, then." He scurried from the kitchen, then returned, looking sheepish, grabbed the pile of rags from the counter and left the room.

Gavin pursed his lips, then stepped aside as another one of the boys barged through the door carrying an armload of dishes. "Well done, Mr. Sharp." He rolled up his sleeves, then turned on the spigot. The scar tissue on his arm tugged, and he rubbed the mangled skin. If he wasn't careful, he'd turn into his father, barking like a rabid dog and demeaning the boys. Fighting wasn't acceptable, but Isobel was right in her assessment of the situation. His father had been anything but firm and loving, and if it wasn't for his secondary-level teacher, Mr. McKay, Gavin might be looking at life through prison bars. The man had come alongside him and converted Gavin's bitterness and anger into acceptance of his father's manner, reminding Gavin he was his own man and could choose to be different, yet these many years later, his father's specter still surfaced. Would Gavin never be free from the man's influence?

A Lesson in Love

Chapter Eleven

"You sent for me, sir, I mean, Mister—Owen." Isobel stood in the doorway to the earl's library, pulse tripping. She had nothing to fear; the man had been gracious and approachable since she'd arrived, but his position in society required deference, an understanding of her place in the caste system called the peerage. She fought the urge to curtsy, instead locking her knees and gripping the doorframe. "Is something wrong?"

He raised his head from the open ledger on the massive desk and smiled. "Ah, Miss Turvine. Thank you for coming so quickly." He motioned to a maroon brocade Queen Anne chair. "Please, have a seat."

She licked her lips and strode across the room, then dropped into the chair. Slightly worn, the cushions eased the throbbing in her back. If she never saw another potato, she'd be happy. "Is something wrong?" she repeated.

"No. Quite the opposite." The earl sat back and steepled his fingers. "You Land Army gals are doing a smashing job, and I'd like to discuss plans to take us through the winter and into next season."

"Next season? You don't think the war will be over by Christmas as everyone says?"

"We're in for a long and bloody war, Miss Turvine. Hitler is not going to roll over, and we must be honest with ourselves. His Luftwaffe and U-boats are running over us to say nothing of the Desert Fox in Africa. The man is a military genius. They've had years to prepare, and we have to catch up before we can defeat him. I know we can, but it won't be easy. Now that the Americans are in the mix, perhaps the war will end sooner than anticipated, but not by much. And we must do our bit to feed the troops, our Allies, and our own people."

Isobel nodded. "We're honored to serve in this way."

"Excellent." He removed his spectacles and tossed them on the desk. "I've made a request for more WLA gals for the 1943 season, so you'll have to make do with the ones you have through the winter."

"That won't be a problem. In fact, I thought we'd be demobbed by November. You expect us to remain with you through the winter?"

"Yes, I'd like to experiment with a few ideas." His eyes sparkled, and he rubbed his hands together. "One growing season isn't enough, and I've been reading about the work of an American, a professor at the University of California. Dr. William Gerike conducted studies in the nineteen twenties with something called hydroponics. Strange word, yes? It's Greek and literally means water-working. He grows produce without soil."

"Without soil?" Isobel straightened. "How is that possible? Where would we do this? If soil isn't required, are you thinking of bringing the plants inside?"

He grinned like a child who'd been presented with a smorgasbord of confections. "Exactly. I knew you'd follow my line of thought. The trick will be to manage the temperature of the room and the sunlight." He pointed to a stack of thick volumes. "There's been extensive research on the topic, and we should consider multiple approaches. Are you with me, Miss Turvine?"

"Absolutely. I'm highly intrigued." She tilted her head. "Have you discussed this with Headmaster Emerson? This project could teach the students the scientific method as well as biology, botany, chemistry, and a host of other topics that escape me at the moment."

"A teacher at heart, aren't you?"

Isobel shrugged. "I didn't mean to overstep."

"You're not. A partnership could be just the thing to get the lads engaged. Learning by doing. However, let's not say anything for the moment. We have much to study and prepare. Please take the books with you and review them. Meanwhile, I'd like to discuss planting winter wheat after the potato harvest is complete. What do you know about that particular crop?"

"Very little, sir, but Tracey and several of the others who are born-and-bred farm girls can guide us. I'll get with them straight away. Have you already made inquiries about where we can obtain seeds?"

"The idea only just came to me, but I'll check with the ministry." The earl pursed his lips, then cleared his throat. "I also wanted to discuss the school. I'm aware of some of the, shall we say, incidents. My initial concerns were about tearing up my property and turning it into a farm, but you ladies have done a brilliant job, and you've kept your quarters clean and undamaged. I can't say the same about the boys. I'm beginning to regret my decision to house them. I've committed to all three terms, but I'm still considering whether they will return after next summer."

"He's…I mean, the teachers are doing the best they can, and the boys' behavior has improved. Last week's dinner, for example. It's still early. We're not even through first term, so they don't have their feet under them yet."

"How long does it take?"

"Normally? At least through the end of the term, but these poor boys have been uprooted from their families and sent to a strange place. They need time to adjust. I hope you'll wait until at least the spring solstice to make your decision."

"Spring solstice?" His face darkened. "I'm not making any promises."

Isobel squirmed in the chair. "Of course not, but I do believe they've made progress. Perhaps if they spent more time with us. If we tire them in the fields, they'll have less energy to get into trouble. We're not their mothers, but a woman's touch can often tame an unruly young man. Also, if they got to know you, they might have more respect for your property. You have a lifetime of experiences to share." She fell silent and nibbled her lower lip.

"You'll need to negotiate your ideas about using the boys with Mr. Emerson, but I've no interest in teaching on a regular basis. And those lads need to improve their behavior because it's the right thing to do, not because of any so-called relationship with me."

"Understood."

His face softened. "I'm not trying to be harsh with them, Miss Turvine, and I don't need to tell you there's a war on, but we don't have the luxury of mollycoddling the boys. Sometimes, one must grow up quickly, and this is such a time." He pulled out his pocket watch. "Now, if you'll excuse me, I have several calls to make."

She jumped to her feet. "Yes, sir, um, Owen." She hurried toward the door.

"Miss Turvine, the books."

Turning on her heel, she huffed out a breath. The man must think her an imbecile. "Yes." She returned to the desk and grabbed the stack of books. "I'll get right on these."

"See that you do." He picked up the telephone receiver and began to dial. "And close the door on your way out."

As she strode down the corridor toward the front door, Isobel cradled the books close to her chest. Had something happened? Granted, her interactions with the earl had been few, but he'd never been as abrupt with her or about the school. An image of young Harry's face floated into her mind as she stepped outside into the sunshine. The boy had made great strides. What would uprooting him again do to the lad? To any of the students? And what about their headmaster? She'd miss the man more than she cared to admit, something she dared not think about.

A Lesson in Love

Chapter Twelve

Isobel threw back the covers, swung her legs over the side of the bed, and poked her feet into her slippers. Yawning, she looked around the room at the other girls. Three still slept, while a couple were propped against their pillow reading. Margery gave her a sleepy smile as she sat up. Isobel whispered, "Church?"

Margery nodded, and Tracey waved. It would be nice to have company on this chilly October morning. She'd attended alone the last three weeks, most of the girls choosing to rest their weary bodies each Sunday after six days of dawn-to-dusk work in the fields. Not that she wasn't bone-tired, but the pastor's sermons invigorated her. A mixture of encouragement and exhortation, the lessons remained with her through the week as she sought to live by example for the young women in her charge.

Shuffling to the bathroom, she let out another yawn. She washed her face and brushed her teeth, and her grogginess dissipated. A muted knock sounded, and she opened the door. Margery leaned against the wall in the corridor. "Tell me again why I'm going with you?"

With a snicker, Isobel patted her friend's shoulder. "You'll be glad you did."

"I know, but at the moment, my mattress holds more allure than a hard pew. I'd give a week's wages for a cushion."

"It's not that bad." Isobel smiled. "Now, get cracking. The wagon pulls out in thirty minutes."

Muttering under her breath, Margery entered the bathroom and shut the door.

Isobel grinned. More bluff than bark, her friend had never enjoyed mornings, one of the reasons Isobel had been stunned at her suggestion they join the Land Army. The girls rose before the birds, often arriving at the fields before light. She shook her head and tiptoed back to the dormitory-style room. Tracey was dressed, her face bright and eyes sparkling. She, on the other hand, embraced morning hours and sprang from her bed ready to attack each day. Her friends couldn't be more different, but she didn't know what she'd do without either one of them.

"Need help hitching the wagon?" Tracey smoothed her skirt, then picked up her leather-bound Bible. "I already ate."

"Of course you did." Isobel shook her head. "Exactly how long have you been up?"

Tracey grinned. "Long before you, missy."

"I'll take care of the wagon. Wouldn't want to muss your outfit, would we?"

"This old thing?" Her friend's eyes sparkled, and she flushed. "Hardly."

"Hmm. Methinks you've got someone you're trying to impress." Isobel tapped her index finger on her chin. "Someone from town? One of the teachers? Who could it be?"

"No one." Tracey's cheeks darkened from pink to red. "There's no one special."

"Lying's a sin, you know," Ethel called from the bed. "I've seen how you turn into a simpering schoolgirl around Mr. Stillwater."

"I do not. He's—"

Isobel held up her arms. "I didn't mean to start a row."

Tracey sagged against the frame of the bunk bed. "Sorry, it's just that I didn't think anyone noticed. I'm a bit embarrassed, truth be told. He's much too old for me. And he doesn't know I exist."

"Bah, age is just a number. And he'd be lucky to have you." Isobel exchanged a glance with Ethel. "Guess we'll have to do something to get his attention."

"Don't you dare," Tracey sputtered. "Now, this discussion of my love life, or lack thereof, is over."

Ethel guffawed. "For now."

Isobel wrapped her arm around Tracey's and said in a stage whisper, "She's just jealous you saw him first."

"Yeah, that's what it is." Pretending to throw her book at them, Ethel grinned. "Don't you have somewhere to be?"

With a squeal, Isobel looked at her watch. "Yes, and we're going to be late if we don't get a move on." She hurried out of the room, Tracey on her heels. They left the house and rushed toward the barn. Once inside,

A Lesson in Love

she was greeted by the earthy odors she'd come to appreciate. Snuffling from the horses and cows mingled with the soft bleating of the goats. She laid her Bible and pocketbook on the warped board that served as the front seat on the wagon, then grabbed the tack from the wall. In moments, she'd managed to hitch the gentle mare to the wagon.

"Our city girl has come a long way." Tracey clapped her hands. "Admittedly, I was skeptical when we met. Figured you'd be as useful as an ant at a summer picnic."

"Me, too." Isobel laughed. "I was sure I'd made the worst decision of my life. Goes to show you." She motioned toward the wagon. "Your chariot awaits, miss. Hopefully, Margery will be ready by the time we pull up to the cottage."

With practiced motions, Tracey pulled her skirt above her knees and scrambled into the wagon, then dropped onto the seat. Isobel climbed up beside her and picked up the reins. What would her parents think of their daughter driving a horse-drawn wagon and leading an army of farm girls? Hopefully, they'd be proud. She clicked her tongue, and the wagon lurched forward. As they exited the barn, a dilapidated bus rumbled up to the front of the manor. Where had that come from?

The door to the bus popped open at the same time as the front door of the house. Jostling and laughing among themselves, a dozen or more of the students hurtled down the steps, followed more slowly by Mr. Stillwater, a teacher whose name Isobel didn't know, and Gavin. She frowned. Had Gavin purchased the vehicle? Surely it didn't belong to the earl who seemed ready to boot the school off his property, if their conversation two weeks ago was any indication.

Where would Gavin have secured the money for such a purchase? To say nothing of the petrol required to operate the vehicle. Had the school received special ration points? She'd never owned a car, so hadn't bothered to learn the system implemented in the months after war had been declared. Isobel's lips twisted. Since when did the British government need her help in managing the ration program? She flicked her wrists, gently slapping the mare's hindquarters, and the horse broke into a trot. The sooner she got to church, the sooner she could focus on something other than the handsome headmaster, who seemed to crowd her thoughts no matter how hard she tried to ignore him.

A plume of acrid exhaust shot out from behind the bus as it rumbled to a stop in front of the manor as Gavin descended the steps. The lads skipped and ran, elbowing each other in their fight to be first onto the vehicle. He should correct their behavior, but none of them seemed in danger of injury, so he exchanged a shrug with Stillwater.

Gravel popped as one of the farm wagons rolled down the lane from the barn toward the cottages that housed the WLA. Heads close together and chatting, Isobel and Tracey sat on the front seat, if the warped wooden board could be called such. The vehicle stopped in front of one of the tiny buildings as its door opened, and several women hurried outside. Like a bouquet of tulips, their colorful dresses brightened the scenery.

Laughing, they scrambled into the back of wagon. He grinned to himself when he realized Isobel was driving, and the memory of their first meeting floated into his mind. She'd come a long way in the two months since she'd arrived.

His pulse thrummed as the wagon continued its journey. They would pass the bus on their way off the estate. The lads poked their heads out the windows of the bus and waved. "Hi, Miss Turvine! Hi, Miss Vincent!"

The women returned the boys' greetings, but Isobel looked at him with a mixture of curiosity and censure. What had he done to earn her displeasure?

"Off to church, are you?" He tucked his hands into his pockets. "That's where we're going as well."

Her gaze flicked toward him but held none of its usual warmth. "Yes."

"That bus has seen better days," Tracey smirked and rubbed her hands together. "I think ol' Buttercup here has a better chance of making it there than your mode of transportation."

He grinned. "Care to make a wager on that, Miss Vincent?"

Her jaw gaped in an exaggerated expression of shock, but her eyes sparkled. "Gambling about going to church, Mr. Emerson? Shame on you."

With a chuckle, he shook his head. "I stand corrected, and I should have offered to take you ladies.

"If that bus proves its worth, perhaps we'll cadge a lift next week. For now, we'll take our chances with the mare."

"Fair enough." He looked at Isobel who'd sat ramrod straight on the bench, facing away from him. She was obviously upset about something, but now was not the time to discuss what he'd done. "See you there."

"We'll save you some seats right next to us, won't we, Isobel?"

Without a glance, Isobel said, "I'm sure there will be plenty of seating for Mr. Emerson and his students."

Tracey gave him an apologetic smile as she shrugged. The wagon lurched forward, and the women waved again at the boys.

Gavin climbed onto the bus with a sigh. Was Isobel annoyed that they'd stopped for conversation? Was she irritated at something that had happened between her and Tracey? One of the other women? Had he done or said something? He tried to recall their recent interactions. There'd been but a few, and all had seemed innocuous. Intriguingly, the boys had enjoyed their time in the field, so had asked to help on two more occasions. He'd worked close by her, but there had been little conversation, although she seemed to enjoy his company.

"Mr. Emerson, are you sweet on Miss Turvine?" A voice piped up from the back of the bus as he dropped into an empty seat.

He whipped his head around to find most of the boys gazing at him in expectation, and a knowing expression on Stillwater's face. "What gave you that idea?"

"So, you don't deny it?" Stillwater chuckled. "That should be our first clue."

Harry tilted his head as the bus rocked and swayed on the pothole-scarred road. "You're always looking at her even when you're talking to someone else. And those times in the field, you made sure to work in the row next to hers. She's nice. I like her. Don't you?"

"She is nice, Harry. I'm glad you noticed that. All of the women have been good to us."

"Yes, but she's like a mom, you know, firm but not mean. And she knows our names. Not all the women do. Some of them call us 'boy.' Can't be bothered, I guess." Harry crossed his arms. "But she knows our names, and she hugs us."

"I like when she does that." Ernie, one of the youngest of the students, beamed. "Do you know if she has any children, Mr. Emerson? She must miss them if she does. Maybe that's why she hugs us."

"I don't know if she has any children, Ernie." Gavin glanced out the window at the yellowing leaves, relieved the conversation had turned from his feelings about Isobel to the woman herself. A kind and caring soul, she'd worked her way into the boys' hearts, perhaps taking the sting out of missing their parents. "She hugs you because she likes you."

Gavin swallowed a sigh. She'd make a wonderful mother. He knew she was single, but was she widowed? That thought had never occurred to him. He assumed she'd never married. She'd talked about losing her parents but never about a husband. Had she kept that to herself? Surely, one of the other girls would have mentioned a husband by now.

Some of them talked about their own: what armed forces' branch they served in, when they'd last heard from them, or how they'd lost their lives.

Ernie's lower lip trembled. "I miss my mum."

The boys looked somber, and Gavin's heart clenched. "We all do, Ernie, even me. No matter how old one is, he holds a special relationship with his mother."

"I'll be glad when this war is over, Mr. Emerson."

"So will I, Ernie, so will I." Gavin squinted out the window. Although, once the conflict was over, he and the enigmatic Isobel Turvine would go their separate ways. Not a thought he relished, but it was for the best. Rubbing the puckered skin on his arm, he frowned. He was a scared schoolteacher who had little to offer a woman of her caliber. His father was right. Marriage was not in the cards for him.

A Lesson in Love

Chapter Thirteen

Rain thrummed on the umbrella as Isobel huddled underneath the protective fabric and hurried along the lane that led from her cottage to the manor. With the exception of chores associated with the animals, the women had been trapped inside for two days. Initially enjoying the reprieve, they'd read, written letters, played cards and games, and caught up on sleep, but this morning had dawned with yet another deluge causing no little amount of crankiness. When Gavin had telephoned to ask if she or one of the other girls might provide a guest lecture on agriculture, she'd jumped at the chance.

Halfway across the estate, she was beginning to change her mind. She shivered as cold water streamed down the back of her slicker and into her oxfords. She'd clearly selected the wrong shoes for her journey. Waders would have been a better choice on this stormy October morning. Tracey and Margery had both waggled their eyebrows at her but remained mute when she notified them of her destination. She didn't bother to respond to their silent comments.

Thunder rumbled, but thankfully no lightning followed. She hated lightning. The unexpected flash. The jagged dagger that shot toward earth eager to do its damage. She understood the science behind the giant spark of electricity, but that didn't mean she had to like it.

Isobel tightened her grip on the handle and increased her pace. Moments later, she hurried up the steps and under the portico that graced the front of the manor. With quick motions, she opened and closed the umbrella several times to shed as much water as possible. As she turned toward the mansion, the massive wooden door swung open, and Gavin stood on the threshold looking dapper in his gray tweed jacket over the pristine white shirt and charcoal-gray slacks. His gray eyes crinkled at the edges as he smiled at her.

Her breath caught. Why did he have to be so handsome? On someone else, all that gray would make them appear somber, like a character out of a Dickens novel, but instead, Gavin looked distinguished, the white hair at his temples giving him a regal air. The only thing missing was a pipe. The thought made her giggle, and his face brightened further.

"Perhaps I should come in through the kitchen rather than traipsing all this water into the foyer."

"Nonsense." He motioned toward the coat-tree and a crate in the corner. "Let me help you out of your slicker, then you can remove your shoes and stow them in the box with the brolly. I'm sorry I don't have a pair of slippers for you."

"You'll allow me in your classroom in stocking feet?" She pressed a hand against her chest in mock astonishment. "What sort of place are you running?"

He chuckled, then motioned for her to pivot so he could grasp the shoulders of her raincoat. "Not Oxford, that's for certain."

Isobel slipped out of the garment and grinned. "What a blessing."

"Not a high-brow are you?" He plucked her broad-brimmed hat from her head, then hung both the jacket and the fedora on the coat-tree.

She sat down on the carved wooden bench and untied her shoes, then toed off the soggy footwear. Fortunately, there were no holes in her wool socks. "Hardly." She rubbed her arms, then stood. "Ready when you are."

"We're in the ballroom."

"But I'm not dressed for a formal affair."

"Cute." He nudged her shoulder as they tramped down the corridor. "I decided to take advantage of the situation and combined all the classes."

Her steps stuttered, then she raised one eyebrow. "My rates just went up."

Gavin threw back his head and guffawed, the laughter bouncing off the walls. His eyes sparkled, and his teeth flashed. "You are a cheeky one. I'll have to speak with the headmaster, and I hear he can be difficult."

Tamping down her racing pulse, she wagged a finger at him. "Now who's the cheeky one? And you're right about the headmaster. Difficult is an understatement."

"I'm sure some of my teachers would agree." He sobered up with a shrug. "But I'm not here for the friendships. Our goal is to provide an excellent education for these lads and to act as their guardians until they can be safely returned to their families."

"You're doing a fine job, and you can't expect to please all your staff. Most of the complainers at my school were those who didn't want to put in the effort." She raised her hand to pat him on the shoulder, then drew back. "Besides, it's about the boys, and they seem to love you. You're the right combination of firm, fair, and friendly."

They arrived at the ballroom, and he motioned to the immense room where the buzz of conversation filled the air. "Perhaps that should be our slogan."

She squared her shoulders as she entered the room. The sixty or so boys fell silent as she and Gavin approached the table near the front. A chalkboard was propped on an easel near the front windows where rain sheeted the glass panes, blurring the scenery outside.

Gavin laced his fingers and smiled at the group. "Well done, lads. I didn't have to call you to attention. Thank you for showing Miss Turvine the respect she deserves. You have all worked hard over these last weeks and learnt bits and pieces about botany and agriculture while you sowed and planted the fields, but I thought you might enjoy a change of pace, and Miss Turvine has agreed to give you the nuts and bolts, as it were, about running a farm. She's had to learn from the ground up, pardon the pun, and has much to share. Pay close attention. There will be a test."

A slight groan rose from the boys, and Isobel wasn't sure if it was because of the man's bad joke or the promise of an exam. He clapped his hands, and the students fell silent. "Miss Turvine, you have the room."

With a deep breath, she nodded, then faced the boys. "Like you lads, I'm a student. I had to learn how to do my job. My friend suggested we join the Land Army. Frankly, I thought she was daft." As a ripple of laughter went through the room, she grinned, and the tension slipped from her shoulders. "I'm from London. What did I know about growing anything? But my other friend, Miss Gillam, is the best and drew alongside me. I've made mistakes, but fortunately nothing irreparable. Do I know everything yet? Not by a long shot, but I've got a great bunch of gals who help me. Collaboration has been key to our success with this assignment."

Warming to her subject, she picked up a piece of chalk and motioned to the slate. "First, let's make a list of skills you think might be necessary to running a farm. Call them out."

"Driving."

"Lifting heavy things."

"Mechanical."

"Good with animals."

"Telling people what to do."

Another round of laughter followed this, and she chuckled as she scribbled down the phrase, the chalk squeaking against the board. More words came, and she continued to write. When silence blanketed the group, she laid down the chalk and brushed the dust from her hands. "Excellent work, gentlemen. Now, raise your hand if you have one of these abilities."

All the boys lifted their arms.

"Two?"

Hands remained in the air.

"Three?"

Some of the students lowered their arms.

"Four?"

More hands fell.

Isobel smiled at the lads, her gaze moving from one face to the next. "I didn't do that to embarrass you or to point out your limitations. I wanted to make my point that we all have a specific set of talents. Some of us do one thing very well. I know how to—how did you put it—tell people what to do. My friend Miss Gillam can drive the tractor and plant. Miss Vincent has learnt how to milk the cows, and she's the fastest one of all. And when we collaborate, each of us doing what we do best, the work gets done.

"Now, as to the specific work, we have two areas of focus here: the produce and the animals. We had to prepare the fields, tearing out the grass, then turning the soil before we created the rows for planting. God sends us sun and rain to ensure things grow, then it will be up to us to harvest at the right time. Meanwhile, we'll take care of the animals by feeding them and cleaning up after them as necessary. They will give us eggs and milk as a result. Each of the tasks I've mentioned entails many steps—"

"Miss Turvine, do you really think God is in charge of the sun and rain? My father says He turned His back on us after He made the world.

That He set things going, then walked away. That's got to be right, otherwise there wouldn't be a war on."

"Mr. Corrigan—"

"It's quite all right, Mr. Emerson." Isobel held up her hand. "God loves questions, Mr. Corrigan, because He knows you're searching for answers." She smiled at the red-faced young man in the third row. "I believe God is involved in every bit of our lives even when it doesn't seem like it, especially now. But He has His fingers in everything from helping our crops grow to guiding us in our daily walk. He cares about all His creation from the chickens scrabbling in the dirt for seeds to you and me. We are all special in His eyes. And we can talk more about that later, just the two of us." She pointed at the list of phrases on the chalkboard. "For now, I'm going to tell you how each of these skills is used here."

She glanced at Gavin, and her stomach fluttered as if a swarm of hummingbirds had taken flight. His expression held a mixture of admiration and something else she couldn't read. She'd jumped at the chance to return to the classroom, but this would be the first and last time at Flagler Manor. She had a job to do, and it didn't include working with the devastatingly handsome headmaster. Because whether or not she was willing to admit it, she was quickly falling for the man, but she could only count on misery to follow. Now, to get through the next hour with her heart intact.

A Lesson in Love

Chapter Fourteen

Hands shoved into his pockets, Gavin strolled across the lawn. Only midmorning, but the unseasonably hot day sent trickles of perspiration down his back. He had papers to grade and lectures to prepare, but the sun had beckoned him from behind the desk as its rays poured through the window and puddled onto the floor next to his chair.

The sound of laughter floated toward him, and he pivoted. Hand blocking the glare from his eyes, he peered toward the area of the estate that had been converted to fields. Even though it was Saturday, the Land Army girls prepared another portion of land for next season. The women worked seven days a week, but most didn't seem to mind the relentless schedule.

His gaze bounced among the crew's bent figures, looking for one in particular. Standing near a wooden cart, Isobel gesticulated wildly as she spoke to one of the women whose name he couldn't remember. The brim of her hat blocked her face, so he couldn't tell if she was angry or excited. Then she threw back her head and laughed. The other woman joined her in merriment. Their joy brought a smile to his lips. They had to be exhausted from the heavy physical labor, yet they'd taken a moment to share some fun. When was the last time he'd done the same?

Filled with class preparation, teaching, and the plethora of administrative tasks associated with being headmaster, his days blurred together one after the other. Each night he tumbled into bed, his mind reviewing the day's activities before finally falling asleep.

Snippets of yesterday's presentation Isobel had made to the lads pushed their way into his head. Although she hadn't admitted it, she'd been nervous. She'd licked her lips repeatedly, and the pulse in her neck fluttered. After she started talking, she'd relaxed, and her eyes were especially bright during her exchange with Calvin Corrigan. Afterward, she'd drawn the lad aside, and they'd chatted for nearly thirty minutes. As he left the room, the boy's expression had been resolute and reflective.

There was definitely a void in the world of education while Isobel was doing her bit to provide food for the troops. Any child would be lucky, no, blessed to be one of her students, but her days at the manor were plenty full without adding teaching. He couldn't give in to the temptation to ask her to guest lecture again. Too bad, because Mr. Martin could learn a thing or two if he bothered to observe her. The man seemed to only go through the motions, his presentations wooden and uninspiring. He was brilliant, an expert in his field, but he seemed better suited to a solitary profession.

Before he could get caught staring, Gavin turned on his heel and continued across the grassy expanse. If he were honest with himself, he too could learn from the beautiful woman. She'd been unapologetic about her faith, weaving her beliefs through the lecture to combine the what and how with the Who and why. He was also a believer, and had been since just before entering secondary school, but he'd allowed his father's constant chastising that a proper gentleman didn't try to proselytize his family and friends to silence his enthusiastic sharing about the change in his life. Eventually, Gavin had begun to believe the rhetoric and stuffed his faith into a back pocket, something to be taken out at *appropriate* times.

He shook his head. That stopped now. As he walked, he prayed, "Forgive me, Lord. I'm no better than the Apostle Peter who denied you three times. I let others dictate my actions when it's You I should answer to and stand up for."

A simple prayer, but warmth filled him which had nothing to do with the heat of the day. God heard him and granted his request. Gavin couldn't decide whether to fall on his face in gratitude or shout to the world. "Thank you, Father." His steps lighter, he nearly sprinted toward the manor. An idea sprang into his head, and he chuckled. Would the boys think him barking mad? Perhaps, but he would take a page from Isobel's book and walk beside his students instead of some perceived notion of being above them.

Once inside the massive home, he wandered into the ballroom where tables had been set up with board games, puzzles, and cards. A handful of boys worked a jigsaw, and he strolled toward them. Glancing at the photo of an aerial dogfight, he frowned. He'd replace the war-themed puzzles in the future, but for now he'd divert the lads' attention. "Good morning, gentlemen."

Startled, they bolted upright. "Sir!"

"Relax, I hope you don't mind the interruption, but I'm of the mind to do some fishing and thought some of you might like to come along."

Peter Donovan, a fourth-year student gaped at him as his former foe, Warren Sharp, cocked his head. "Fishing, sir?"

Maybe not barking mad, but the lads were definitely stumped at his suggestion. Gavin stifled a smile. "Don't worry, lads, I'm as surprised as you at the offer. A Londoner, I'm not exactly the outdoor type, but the day is beautiful, and I'd like to spend time with you. Not lecturing, not telling you what to do, just a group of men trying their hand at something new. What say you?"

Iain Nettleton crossed his arms. "I'm game, sir. How about some friendly competition? Whoever catches the most fish gets a day off from school."

Gavin chuckled. "Does that include me, Iain?"

"Sure, why not?" The boy shot him a cheeky grin. "Of course, you'll have to get that approved by the headmaster."

"That could be tough."

"Nah, he's a right good bloke once you get to know him."

Clapping the young man on the back, Gavin swallowed the lump that had formed in his throat. "Let's get to it, then, shall we? What I know about fishing fits on the head of a pin, but I've heard worms are the required bait. Let's head to the fields and see if Miss Turvine and her ladies have any extra."

"She's a corker. Maybe she could go with us."

"That she is, boys, and you can ask, but she might need to keep working."

They trooped out of the manor, then hurried toward the fields. Iain broke into a run, and the other students followed suit. By the time Gavin arrived, the boys were explaining their mission.

Isobel raised her gaze to his, her face a mixture of amusement and admiration. "So, you're going fishing."

"Yes, well—"

"I think it's a splendid idea."

"You do? Because other than time with the boys, I'm beginning to regret my impulsive decision. In fact, all we've done thus far is come to you looking for worms. I haven't checked with the earl about fishing rods or other equipment that might be necessary."

She snickered. "What's this? A man admitting his shortcomings? You never cease to amaze me, Mr. Emerson. But you are in luck. Fishing is one of Tracey's favorite pastimes, and she has all the gear you could possibly need."

He huffed out an exaggerated breath. "That's a relief. I don't suppose she could come along to show us what to do."

"I'm afraid not. It's all hands on deck today, but you're an intelligent man as are your students." Her eyes twinkled with suppressed merriment. "You can do this, and we'll expect fish on the menu."

"For the lot of us? That's a tall order."

"No, it's not, Mr. Emerson. Besides, I plan to win the competition. I'm going to catch a whole boatload of fish," Warren said.

Isobel's left eyebrow rose, and she leveled her gaze on Gavin. "A wager?"

"A contest. The winner gets a day off from classes." Gavin motioned toward the ground, then scoffed. "I've just realized we didn't bring a pail or anything to collect the worms. I really am hopeless, aren't I?"

"Give yourself some grace, Mr. Emerson. It is, after all, your first fishing excursion." She pointed to a stack of bushel baskets. "Grab one of those and put some dirt in it. Your worms will never realize they haven't left home."

"Thanks, Miss Turvine," Peter said before trotting toward the stack.

Iain dropped to his knees a short distance away and began to dig in the freshly turned soil. Seconds later, he whooped and held up three wriggling worms. "Found 'em!"

Gavin shrugged. "And the game is afoot."

"Good luck, Sherlock," Isobel said, before she beamed at Iain. "Well done, Iain."

Gavin beckoned to the other students and made his way to Iain. "Apparently, he's found the motherlode, boys. Shouldn't take us long."

Another holler, and Warren tossed a worm into the dirt-filled basket. "Come on, Mr. Emerson. You're missing the thrill of the hunt."

"Indeed." He knelt next to Peter and pushed his hands into the dirt. The scar tissue on his arm tugged, but he ignored the pull and exchanged a smile with the young man. "Thanks for your willingness to spend the morning with this old man."

"Thanks for asking us." The boy's cheeks were flushed. "We, um, try to be brave, but we miss doing stuff like this with our fathers. Not that my dad knows one end of a fishing rod from the other, but you know what I mean."

"I do." Gavin cleared his throat and nudged Peter's shoulder with his own. "No matter what our age, we miss our fathers when they're not around." Where had that sentiment come from? He had few happy memories of his childhood or his father, but in a tiny corner of his heart, if he were honest, his father's absence left a void. And now, Gavin had the chance to be a surrogate father to his students, a responsibility he hadn't considered when taking the job. What a precious opportunity. He'd spend extra time in prayer tonight getting guidance from his heavenly Father.

He glanced at Isobel who was looking in his direction. Grinning, he held up a worm. She giggled, the sound floating toward him like wind chimes. He'd also talk to God about the charming and beautiful Miss Turvine, because whether or not he liked it, she was beginning to take up residence in another part of his heart.

A Lesson in Love

Chapter Fifteen

The rumble of the John Deere enveloped Isobel as she guided the vehicle down the field, a spinner attached to the back of the machine. The time had finally come to harvest the main crop potatoes, and the entire team was at work. She, Tracey, and Margery had the first shift with the tractor, while Ethel, Priscilla, and Nancy used a draft horse attached to another spinner. Did all the WLA troupes have access to more than one of the harvesting tools, or had the earl used his high connections to obtain a second one? No matter the reason, they'd be able to unearth twice as many tubers each day.

She glanced at the sun high overhead, then tugged her hat lower on her face. A light breeze caressed her face, taking the sting out of the day's heat. Once again, a wealth of knowledge, Tracey had coached Isobel that it was best to harvest the potatoes after the foliage had died back and only when the soil temperature was above ten degrees centigrade. The last two days were spent clearing away the tops in order to access the tubers below ground. Her back still ached, and she'd had no problem falling asleep.

Humming a hymn from Sunday's service, she tightened her grip on the wheel and tossed a glance over her shoulder at Tracey and Margery. Tracey grinned and waved. Margery made a comment Isobel couldn't hear above the roar of the engine, and Tracey laughed. Isobel smiled at their frivolity, then turned around to focus on the rows ahead of her. The farmwork had been more grueling than she'd ever imagined when she agreed to sign up for the WLA, but she was making a difference in the war effort. She wasn't building planes or manufacturing ammunition, but she was keeping the troops fed and supplying British Restaurants in London, the communal kitchens created to give people who'd run out of ration stamps or been bombed out a place to cook their meals.

She watched a pair of birds swoop back and forth in the cloudless blue sky. They seemed to be enjoying the beauty of the day rather than hunting for food. The musty odor of the overturned soil mingled with smell of manure. She reached the end of the row and wheeled the tractor into a wide turn, then set the brake and climbed out. She motioned to Tracey, then massaged her lower back. "You're next to drive."

"You sure? I can keep manning the spinner."

"No, I should have swapped out at the end of the last row." Isobel surveyed the field, and her chest swelled. "We've made tremendous progress. If you'd told me we'd harvest several tonnes of potatoes with only a dozen girls, I'd have laughed in your face."

Margery fisted one hand as she bent her arm, then tapped the muscle in her upper arm. "Told you this baby would grow. The lumberjills have nothing on us."

Isobel snickered. "No, and truth be told, I'd rather work the fields than be felling and loading trees onto trains in the wilds of Scotland."

"I second that." Tracey nodded. "All right, break's over." She scrambled onto the tractor, reminding Isobel of their fifteen-year age difference. The young woman's stamina never seemed to flag.

Taking her place next to Margery, Isobel removed her hat, pulled a handkerchief from her pocket, and blotted the perspiration from her face. She donned the broad-brimmed fedora, then tucked her long braid inside the hat. In a cloud of exhaust, the vehicle lurched forward, and she and Margery followed, periodically clearing the spinner of debris. The work was mindless, so she and her friend alternately shouted above the noise in conversation and sang to pass the time.

She looked across the expanse at Ethel's team and shook her head in disbelief. The horse-drawn spinner was keeping pace with the tractor. A huge animal who towered over everyone, the draft horse had initially terrified Isobel, but despite the mare's size of more than 140 stone and herculean strength, she was a gentle as a baby. As if she knew Isobel was looking at her, the horse bobbed her head several times.

Isobel chuckled. "Show off."

"She is, isn't she?" Margery grinned. "Just another one of us girls doing a man's job."

"This has been quite an experience. There are days I question my sanity for about a million reasons, and then I consider all we've done, and all I've learnt, and I realize I'm where I'm supposed to be. At least for the moment." She shrugged. "I didn't think I'd ever leave London."

"Neither did I, but the Jerries made that decision with the Blitz." She tilted her head. "Do you think you'll go back, you know, when the war's over?"

"Why wouldn't I?"

Margery jerked her head toward the lawn on the south side of the manor where the boys were playing cricket. The sound of their cheers and laughter floated toward them, then the crack of the ball against the bat, and Isobel watched as the boy, known as the striker, raced toward the wicket in an attempt to exchange places with his teammate, the non-striker. The fielder dropped the ball, and the cheering grew louder.

"Nice to see the boys outside, although I've never been a big fan of cricket." Margery motioned to the spinner, and they cleared the debris. "I've heard the American game of baseball is much more exciting, but I don't understand the allure of smacking a tiny ball, then chasing it. Kind of like puppies, don't you think?"

Isobel laughed. "Boys and their toys, eh?"

"However, I must say cricketeers look mighty fine in their uniforms. What do the Americans wear?"

"You're a bad one."

"Which is one of the reasons we're friends. I say and do the things you want to."

"Like join an army of women to plant and harvest food?" Isobel massaged her neck. "I don't remember that thought ever entering my mind."

"Ha, beats working in the factories, and you know it. I didn't realize how much I liked being outside. London certainly didn't hold that allure. I might be a farm girl at heart. Who knew?"

"It is nice not to be cooped up. And the scenery is lovely."

"You can say that again." Margery wiggled her eyebrows up and down. "And it has everything to do with a certain tall, dark, and handsome headmaster. I mean he's no Laurence Olivier or Stewart Granger, but he'll do. A couple of the other teachers are also lookers, but he's the most handsome, don't you think? I especially love that graying on his temples. Thankfully, he shed that brooding Heathcliff persona after he met you."

"Margery!"

"What?" Her friend shot her a saucy smile. "I was just saying—"

"You are not saying what I'm thinking." Isobel tugged at her sleeves. "I admit he's attractive, but I'm not in the market for a husband. That ship has sailed. I've carved out a life, and I'm content."

"Content? Who wants to be merely content? No, life should be lived to the fullest, and that includes sharing it with someone who can't breathe they're so in love with you."

"You've been reading too many dime novels or Jane Austen. I'm not sure which." Isobel shook her head. "Besides, he's not given any indication that he's interested in me or any of us. He has a school to run."

"No indication," Margery shrieked. "No indication? Are you daft? His eyes follow you everywhere. He seems to find reasons to interact, and his face lights up when you appear. Mark my words, missy. He's interested."

Isobel's pulse skittered. "Nonsense."

Margery's gaze pierced Isobel. "Don't hesitate like I did and lose out on love. Trust me. You'll never forgive yourself."

Chapter Sixteen

Pinpricks of light dotted the night sky as Isobel sat on the waist-high wall surrounding the cottage. She slipped her hands under her thighs as bats chittered overhead in the darkness. Two days had passed since the last of the potatoes had been harvested. Two days during which the girls had rested and enjoyed time for themselves. Winter wheat was the next crop to sow, and Tracey assured her there was plenty of time to get the seeds into the ground, so Isobel arranged a light schedule for the girls to handle the bare minimum of chores. The weather had cooperated with unseasonable warmth and lots of sunshine.

She'd slept late both mornings, waking long after dawn had broken to find the cottage vacant, then spent the days alternately propped against a tree with a book or lying on a blanket with a book. Always a fast reader, she'd devoured three novels.

While she stayed on the estate, some of the girls had taken the lorry to explore the tiny village a few kilometers away, and the rest had gone hiking on the first day. Today the girls challenged the boys to a game of cricket. Not her idea of recuperation, but to each their own. She'd grown fond of the girls, but the solitude had been refreshing. No one asking questions. No one squabbling. No one wondering where she was or what she was doing.

Gavin had shown up late yesterday afternoon, concern evident on his face as he approached. She'd pretended a nonchalance she didn't feel and impressed herself with the calm manner in which she answered his questions. No, she wasn't ill. No, she hadn't injured herself. Yes, she was right as rain, just reveling in the silence. He'd flushed at the last statement, and she'd assured him she didn't mind the interruption.

Before she could change her mind, she'd invited him to stay, and they'd chatted for nearly three hours, the time passing in the blink of an eye. They studiously avoided discussing the war, instead talking about the boys and their progress, theories of education, and ideas to keep the lads engaged. It had felt good to immerse herself back into teacher mode, reminding her again how much she missed her young students.

Gavin had talked her into another visit to his class, this time to work on their writing skills. She'd tried to tell him that her methods with the primary children wouldn't work with his boys, but he'd insisted that whatever she did would be perfect. She'd reluctantly agreed, and despite her desire to be in the classroom, regretted her decision.

Groaning, Isobel hopped off the wall and began to pace. She'd told herself weeks ago to keep her distance from the attractive headmaster, yet her resolve went out the window every time she saw him. She should have sent him away this afternoon and had only done so when the girls had returned from the cricket game, dirty and perspiring. Margery and Tracey had both sent her knowing looks, then teased her mercilessly at dinner.

Neither believed her protests that they'd merely been talking as educational colleagues.

A cold breeze lifted her hair, and she buttoned her coat against the chill. Another gust, and she sniffed the air. The acrid tang of tobacco smoke wafted toward her. She'd seen several of the teachers striding along the lanes with pipes, chins in the air, and a swagger in their step. The only things missing to complete the lofty picture of distinguished professors were tweed jackets with patches on the elbows. She rolled her eyes. Too many of Gavin's teachers seemed to consider themselves smarter and better than the students and the women. Having seen the same behavior at the secondary school in her district, she wasn't surprised at their smugness.

Clucking sounded from the barn, and she whipped her head toward the noise. The chickens should be asleep. After dinner, Ethel assured her she'd secured the barn door, but if that was the case, Isobel shouldn't hear the birds. As she started to jog toward the building, the clucks became squawks, and high-pitched whinnies followed. Isobel broke into a run. The distinct odor of burning wood filled the air, and she pumped her legs harder. She couldn't risk going back to the cottage to rouse the girls. "Please, God, let me get there in time. Protect those poor beasts and birds."

As she approached the barn, she could see light between the slats and smoke seeping into the night. She yanked open the door and shrieked as the blast of oxygen she'd sent inside fed the flames, causing them to shoot higher. The horses stomped and screamed. She stripped her jacket and wrapped it around her nose and mouth. There was no time to wet the garment, not if she was going to save the animals.

Chickens swirled around her feet as they seemed to sense which direction to flee. She coughed and batted at the gray smog that clouded her vision. The training she'd received at school told her she had two to three minutes before she risked passing out and that crawling on the ground would give her extra time, but with the horses' fear, that option was just as dangerous as the smoke. Time seemed to stand still as she hurried toward the squealing horses as they banged against their stalls. "Easy…girls." *Cough. Cough.* "I'm…coming." *Cough.*

Her lungs burned as if the fire were inside her. Her vision began to swim. *Lord, give me strength.* She stumbled and fell against the door to the enclosure, and the mare reared onto her hind legs, then slammed her hooves to the ground. Isobel's fingers searched for the latch, reaching, scrabbling, then finally curled around the fastener and lifted it open. Heart pounding and dizzy, she held her breath, snatched the coat from her face, and flung it over the horse's eyes. Wordlessly, she tugged on the mare's mane, praying the terrified animal wouldn't crush her. Miraculously, the horse calmed and followed Isobel from the stall.

Smoke enveloped them, and Isobel lost her bearings, tears streaming from her stinging eyes. Where was the door? She swayed, perspiration plastering her blouse to her skin as her knees trembled. Too much time had elapsed. She and the beautiful, hard-working horse were going to perish. "God—"

"Isobel!" A strong arm wrapped itself around her shoulder. "I've got you. Let go of the horse."

She staggered but retained her grip. "No, she'll die." A cough overtook her.

"There's plenty of help. We're all here." Gavin untangled her fingers from the mane. "You need to get out of the barn. Your lungs."

Shouts filled the barn as he swept her into his arms and carried her from the building. Shadowy figures pushed past them, entering the inferno to rescue the other two mares. Fresh air caressed her face, and she tried to suck in a deep breath. Overcome with paroxysms of coughing and gagging, she winced as knifelike pain stabbed her chest. She moaned as Gavin laid her on the ground.

"Isobel, darling." He stroked her cheek, then drew back when she began another coughing fit. He sat her up and supported her back with his arm. He beckoned toward one of the boys standing nearby. "Water! I need water over here!"

Eyes, throat, and lungs burning, she whimpered. Seconds later, he pressed a glass against her lips, and she sipped the tepid liquid. The wetness soothed some of the sting, and she managed to take a raspy breath without coughing or gagging. In the distance, she heard the clanging bells of emergency vehicles. The auxiliary fire service had arrived. Would they be able to save the structure?

The bells got closer, then ceased, and a door slammed. Footsteps thundered toward her, then someone knelt beside her. She cracked one eyelid. An elderly man carrying a black leather bag patted her arm. "Let's take a look at you, miss, then we'll get you to hospital."

"I'm...fine." *Cough.*

"We'll see about that." He opened the bag and took out a torch. "With the fire, I don't have to worry about blackout restrictions. The Jerries can see us for miles if they're looking in this direction. Now, open wide so I can take a peek at your throat."

As the ambulance worker examined her, Isobel realized Gavin hadn't left her side. He cradled her right hand in both of his, rubbing his thumb over the skin in circles. Fear and concern, and something else battled for supremacy in his eyes. He extricated one hand and brushed a stray hair off her forehead. Was it possible he cared as much as Tracey and Margery claimed he did? No, if she appeared as ghastly as she thought, he was merely distraught at her injuries. Yes, that was it. It had to be. Anything else was unimaginable.

Chapter Seventeen

Gavin huddled in the corner of the ambulance as the vehicle sped out of the estate and onto the road on its way to the hospital. Despite the doctor's calm assurance that he believed Isobel's chance for a full recovery was good, Gavin prayed. Worried, then prayed some more. Nothing was a given. He'd known too many over the years who were supposed to live, yet succumbed to illness or injury.

The doctor administered a shot, and Isobel barely seemed to notice. A few minutes later, the lines on her face relaxed. He pulled the blanket over her, then turned to Gavin. "I've given her a sedative, and we'll take blood to check her oxygen level and a chest X-ray to ascertain the extent of her lung damage. She's a brave young lady. Do you know how long she was inside the barn?"

Shaking his head, Gavin said, "I can call the girls after Isobel is settled. They might know."

"No matter. The tests will tell us what we need to know." The doctor dropped onto the bench next to Gavin and rubbed the back of his neck. "I've done all I can until we arrive. She seems to be special to you. Even sedated, she will sense your presence, so why don't you hold her hand and talk to her."

"I, um, that is, she's a work colleague."

One brow raised, the doctor eyed Gavin over his spectacles. "In all my forty-five years in the medical profession, I've never looked at any of my colleagues as you did while our patient was lying on the ground. You may not know it yet, but she means a great deal to you." When Gavin opened his mouth to protest, the man raised his hands. "I've said enough, and it's none of my business."

He pulled out a pocket watch and popped open the cover, then peered out the window at the back of the vehicle. "We're almost there. When we arrive, you'll be asked to remain in the waiting room until we're finished with the examination. Waiting is the worst, but shouldn't be more than thirty minutes. A nurse will retrieve you when you can sit with your young lady... I mean, *colleague*."

Gavin crouched in the space between the two benches and laced his fingers with Isobel's as he studied her face. Her breathing was noisy, and she occasionally coughed, but the doctor had commented earlier that her color was good, which apparently boded well for her. Nonetheless, she had a long road to recovery, and she would be upset about not being able to do her job and lead the girls. He had no doubt her friends Tracey and Margery would step in, and the work would get done. The entire team would work harder to make her proud. He'd seen the way they rallied around her. She'd created a loyal and steadfast group, even among the two ladies who seemed to thrive on bickering.

The vehicle stopped, and Gavin climbed to his feet as the back hatch opened. A burly man in a white lab coat stood beside a gurney as the ambulance worker grabbed the handles of the stretcher. Gesturing for Gavin to pick up the other handles, the doctor said, "Slow and steady, son."

Moments later, the stretcher had been transferred to the wheeled bed, and Isobel was being rolled through the double doors to the medical facility. A nurse laid her hand on Gavin's arm and spoke gently. "She's in good hands. Dr. Bradford is one of the best. He was a surgeon at St. Mary's Hospital until he retired and moved back to Yorkshire."

"Thank you. He said there's a waiting room."

"Yes, sir. Follow me." She led him to a small room off the lobby. "Make yourself comfortable, and I'll bring you some tea straight away. Feel free to use the telephone if there are loved ones you need to notify. After she's settled, we'll worry about paperwork. Care is what's important now."

Numb with worry, Gavin nodded and hurried to phone. How many tiny hospitals in the far reaches of England had the instrument available for patients' families and friends? Was this more of the earl's patronage? He lifted the receiver and mumbled into it. A series of buzzes and clicks, then the earl's voice came over the line. Gavin gave him an update on Isobel, his voice cracking as he said her name.

The earl assured him the fire had been doused, and the animals were safe and being cared for. None of the other girls had been injured, and the auxiliary firemen were finishing up, so he'd left them to do their job after determining the damage had been extensive with half the building reduced to rubble.

"I'm sorry to hear that, sir, I mean, Owen. Do they know what cause the fire?" Gavin held his breath. While the doctor had worked on Isobel, Gavin had gone over numerous scenarios in his head as to how the conflagration could have started, and he kept returning to the same thought, one of his students.

"Yes, well, I was going to wait to tell you, but since you've asked, it was young Mr. Kemp. He snuck into the barn for a smoke, and something startled him. He dropped the cigarette into the hay, and before he knew it, the flames became too much. He scarpered into the woods. We've only just found him."

Gavin's stomach clenched. Harry had made so much progress until now. "I see. What's been done with the lad?"

"He's with me. Mr. Stillwater wanted to confine him in one of the classrooms, but he'll spend the time with me until you return, away from the others. I've got a bedroom where he can sleep. We'll talk."

"Sir, I'm sorry the culprit is one of my students. I should have kept a better eye on him. First, the tractor, and now the barn. This is serious. It will cost you a significant amount of money. I'll be back later and take him. You shouldn't have to handle this." Gavin pinched the bridge of his nose. "In the morning, I'll begin making arrangements for us to relocate, and I'll look into getting you reimbursed for the damage."

"Boys will be boys. Yes, Harry should have known better, but this wasn't malicious. I haven't decided about the consequences. You and I will discuss that, but don't give another thought to moving the school. I've rather got used to having you and the lads around."

Shoulders sagging, Gavin leaned against the wall. What had changed the man's mind? "Are you sure?"

"Quite. Now, take all the time you need seeing about our Miss Turvine."

"Will do. Goodbye, sir."

"Goodbye."

Gavin hung up the phone, crossed his arms, and bowed his head. He was sure the earl would throw them out as a result of the fire and report them to the Ministry of Works. At least, not having to find a new location was one less crisis to deal with. Intriguingly, the man hadn't seemed angry about the ruination of the barn.

"Mr. Emerson?"

His head whipped up, and he bolted upright. "Yes?"

A nurse stood in the doorway. "The doctor has said you may visit with Miss Turvine for a few minutes, then she must get her rest. She's woozy, but she shouldn't talk much anyway. The X-ray indicates her lungs are in good shape, but the blood test results won't be available until tomorrow. We're giving her oxygen as a precaution." She beckoned him. "Follow me."

He strode across the room, then followed the petite woman down the corridor. They turned into one of the dormitory-style rooms, and he spied Isobel on a bed in the far corner. He suppressed the desire to race past the nurse and gather Isobel in his arms. She must have heard their footsteps because she turned her head, then gave him a wan smile. His pulse tripped.

After what felt like an eternity, he was at her side. He dragged the wooden ladder-back chair close to the bed, then dropped onto its hard seat.

"Five minutes, Mr. Emerson."

"Yes, ma'am."

The woman walked away on soundless feet. She'd make an excellent cat burglar.

Before he could change his mind, Gavin drew her hand into his. "How are you feeling?"

"Tired. So very tired." Her voice came out as a ragged whisper.

"Not in pain?"

"Some, but they've given me something." She coughed, then shook her head. "I—"

"Don't talk." He tossed a look at the desk where the nurse sat. "Clara Barton down there will have my head if you end up with a coughing fit."

She giggled, and her color improved.

He grinned, then sobered. "I've spoken with the earl. Harry is the one responsible for the fire. He was smoking in the barn."

"Oh, no."

"Yeah, I don't what to do with him." Gavin sighed. "He's with the earl now. They're going to talk. It's amazing. Sir Flag—I mean, Owen, wasn't upset. He lost half his barn, and he didn't sound the least bit angry. You know what he said? Boys will be boys? Who says that after one of his buildings nearly burns to the ground? I had no indication Harry had started to smoke. Where is he getting them? Are there other boys smoking?" He tugged at his collar with his free hand. "I need to determine the repercussions."

"Don't be heavy-handed with the lad," she whispered. "I'm sure he feels bad about what happened."

"Even so, he must face the consequences."

"Stop berating yourself. I can hear it in your voice."

"But this is my fault. I'm in charge. It should never have happened."

Isobel squeezed his fingers. "Young people are going to find a way to do what they want. They're clever that way."

"I—"

She extricated her hand and pressed two fingers against his lips. "You are not responsible for this. Harry made a choice. You've done a wonderful job with them." She cleared her throat, then began to cough.

Gavin jumped up and poured water into the glass from the pitcher on the bedside table. Her coughing subsided, and he held the cup to her mouth while supporting her back with one arm. He could feel the nurse's piercing glare without turning around. "Enough talking. I've overstayed my welcome, and you must rest."

After draining the cup, she sighed, and he refilled the glass as she flopped against the pillow. Perspiration dotted her forehead, and he pulled out his handkerchief and blotted the moisture from her skin.

"Pray for me." A sheen of moisture coated her eyes. "I need to make a full recovery." She motioned to her throat. "Talking is my job. What if I can't?"

"Of course I'll pray, but the doctor is very optimistic about your case. Now, close your eyes." He stroked her head. "I'll sit with you until you fall asleep."

A single tear streaked her cheek, and she nodded.

He thumbed away the wetness, the backs of his own eyes prickling at her distress. He returned to the chair and gazed at her face. The nurse had missed a smudge of dirt at Isobel's hairline, and a scratch marred her forehead, but she was beautiful. She'd never believe him if he told her she was pretty. Most women thought beauty had to do with their features, but her true beauty lay inside, and that's what drew him like the clichéd moth to a flame. Rubbing the scar tissue on his arm that still ached from having carried her, he began to pray because it was high time he brought his feelings about the lovely Miss Turvine to his heavenly Father.

Chapter Eighteen

Isobel's eyes fluttered open. Propped against a couple of pillows, she was able to see the bright blue sky through the window across the room. Sunlight poured through the glass as awareness flooded into her mind. Two days had passed since the fire, and she was still in the hospital. She plucked at the sheets and took inventory of her injuries. For the first time since arriving, her throat didn't burn nor did her eyes feel like she'd been in a windstorm on the beaches of Brighton. She took a deep breath, then another. Only a slight twinge. Perhaps the doctor was right and there would be no lasting damage to her lungs. *Please, God, let it be so.*

Footsteps sounded, and her pulse tripped. She recognized Gavin's tread, different from the squeak of the nurses' rubber soles against the gleaming wooden floor. Turning her head, she watched him cross the room.

His face lit when he met her eyes, and he rushed forward. Bending, he placed a hand on her forehead. His smiled widened as he straightened, then dragged the chair closer and dropped onto the seat. "You're looking rather shipshape and Bristol. How are you feeling?"

She giggled. "Better, *Doctor*, but you shouldn't spend time with just one patient."

Cheeks tinged with red, he shrugged. "I may not be a physician, but your color is better, and your eyes don't seem to be clouded with pain. So, in my *professional* opinion, you seem improved."

"In this case, you are correct." Suddenly conscious of her thin hospital gown, she shifted in the bed and pulled the covers under her chin. Fortunately, she was no longer on oxygen, so the tubes which had been hooked over her ears and poked into her nostrils were gone, but the nurses hadn't let her see a mirror, and her hair must be a rat's nest, to say nothing about the scabs on her, yet he looked at her as if she were dressed in her finest. Who was this man? "You don't have to visit every day. You have a school to run."

"I've put Stillwater in charge, and he's enjoying his moment of glory."

"Is he really that bad?"

"No. I struggle with the man's ego, but he's stopped his squabbling with Martin, and he's rallied the other teachers and the boys to buckle down. One small blessing from the fire is that it has matured the lads. They see that pranks and poor decisions sometimes have dire consequences."

"How is Harry? I don't want him to worry about me."

"He wanted to come today, but I said you'd make time for him after you were released. He wants to apologize in person for his foolishness."

"I hope you've not been too hard on him. His guilt about what happened outweighs any punishment you can devise."

"True, and we're not. He's been confined to quarters when not in class or with the earl who has taken Harry under his wing. Both are close-mouthed about their conversations, but the lad seems more confident and serious. According to his teachers, he's beginning to excel in his studies, and I've seen the same in my class. I'm sorry it took this incident to mature him, but he seems to have learnt from it. Not all young men do."

Isobel raised one eyebrow. "There's a story there. We've talked a bit about your childhood when you weren't reading to me, but your stories have been somewhat benign. Did a certain young man take a while to mature?"

Gavin's jaw hardened, and his eyes took on a distant glaze. A long moment passed, then he shook his head and smiled. A forced smile if ever she saw one.

"It appears I've struck a nerve. We can talk about something else." She gestured to the Agatha Christie novel on the bedside table. "Or we can continue with Hercule Poirot's adventures. He still doesn't know the identity of the killer."

He picked up the book and studied the cover, his face still a stony mask. "Perhaps reading. We need to give your throat a rest. Your real doctor will have my head if he discovers how much talking we've been doing. Would you like some water first?"

"That would be lovely. I am parched."

"But not sore?"

"No. God has seen fit to heal me."

"Then He has been gracious enough to hear my prayers, and those of the lads." He returned to book to the table, then rose, and poured water into the glass. "Do you need help?"

She shook her head, then her skin tingled at the memory of yesterday when he wrapped one of his arms around her shoulder to brace her while she drank. Isobel reached for the glass, then sipped the soothing liquid. Hopefully, he didn't notice her trembling hand, and drinking would preclude the need to talk. His nearness scrambled her thoughts and emotions. They were colleagues, and barely that. He was a headmaster and she a teacher turned Land Army girl.

Gavin opened the book where a slip of paper marked their progress. He cleared his throat. "Ready?"

"Yes, but at some point, you are going to have to deal with whatever has soured your mood."

"Now, who's playing doctor?" There was an edge of steel in his voice despite his apparent attempts at levity.

"Not doctor...friend. Someone who has had her own foibles and disappointments over the years. Someone who has learnt that nothing is too burdensome for God to carry on my behalf." She handed him the empty glass, and their fingers grazed. A jolt of electricity shot up her arm, and she licked her lips. Friend, right. "Enough said. Your business is your own. But instead of Hercule's adventures, would you mind reading to me from my Bible?" She had said enough, but perhaps something from God's Word would touch his heart, but was she overstepping? Their friendship was tenuous. Would he resent her interference?

"Not at all." He exchanged the mystery novel for the slim leather-bound volume, then cocked his head. "But why do I think this might be more for me than for you? Do you have a particular section in mind?"

Isobel sent him a saucy smile to lighten the mood. "As a matter of fact, I do. The fifth chapter of second Corinthians, starting with verse fourteen."

To her relief, he chuckled. "Thanks for not starting with verse ten."

She snickered. "Yes, we're going to read about God's love not His judgment."

"Very well." He cleared his throat. "For the love of Christ constraineth us; because we thus judge, that if one died for all, then we're all dead: And that he died for all, that they which live should not henceforth live unto themselves, but unto him which died for them, and rose again. Wherefore henceforth know we no man after the flesh: yea, though we have known Christ after the flesh, yet now henceforth know we him no more. Therefore, if any man be in Christ, he is a new creature: old things are passed away; behold, all things are become new." He raised his head, a rueful smile on his lips. "Point taken, and thanks for the reminder. Too often I hear my father's voice inside my head instead of the Lord's. I am a new man, and the only one I need to please is God."

"I'm sorry your relationship was difficult."

Gavin lifted one shoulder in a half-hearted shrug. "Men like him rarely understand those who are different. He is a professor at Oxford and highly esteemed, whereas I chose to teach secondary school, not nearly as prestigious." He rubbed the scar tissue on his twisted arm. "Coupled with the damage I sustained in the last war, he's made it clear that no woman in her right mind would want a man such as me."

"Oh, Gavi—"

"Forget it. I shouldn't have said anything. I've never told anyone." He waved one hand in a dismissive gesture. "You're supposed to be recovering, not listening to my maudlin ramblings."

"Nonsense. I'm pleased you chose to share with me. It's hard when the opinion of those we love is important to us, and they let us down. But your father is wrong on both topics. You have the opportunity to mold lads like Harry into upstanding young men, and that is very important. And as far as no woman wanting you, that's utter balderdash. You are an intelligent, witty, integrity-filled man of God."

"But my arm—"

Isobel bolted upright. "Is scarred and twisted and perhaps not as strong as the other, but we all have scars, Gavin; most of which can't be seen. As a believer, you are a new creation on the inside, and that's where it counts. Others may have treated you as less because of your injury, but they are wrong. You have value as one of God's children. Don't ever forget that." She flopped back onto the pillow, and if the heat of her face was any indication, her cheeks were bright red. Her throat burned, but she continued, "I've said too much. I'm sorry if I've offended you, but—"

He laid his fingers on her lips for a brief moment. "Hush. Thank you for speaking your mind. You're right, and I've allowed my father's opinion to define me, when I should only have tried to please my heavenly

Father." He sighed, then winked at her, and pointed to the novel. "Now that you've helped me learn my lesson, may we try to solve a mystery?"

Giggling, she nodded. "I guess I need to be more subtle."

"No, ma'am. You're perfect just the way you are."

Her pulse skipped. She'd like to tell him the same thing.

A Lesson in Love

Chapter Nineteen

Gavin strode across the hospital waiting room, reached the window, then pivoted and returned to his original spot. Pivot. Walk. Pivot. Walk. Like the caged leopard he'd seen at the zoo as a child. Now he understood how the poor beast felt. As soon as he arrived, he'd been ushered into the sterile space by a nurse who'd indicated Isobel wasn't finished changing into her clothes. Nibbling the inside of his cheek, he glanced at the clock. A mere ten minutes had passed.

If she were anything like his mum, she'd be a while. Memories of his parents rushed into his head. Attired in a three-piece suit, Father would sit in the parlor behind the newspaper, sighing and mumbling about being late, and still Mother wouldn't appear. Then she'd come down the stairs and into the opulent room, the fabric of her gown swishing as she glided across the floor. He'd harrumph and make a big deal about laying aside the paper, but the look on his face always belied his anger. His eyes would brighten as he rose and extended his arm, adoration on his face, the antithesis of the man he became after Mum's death, constantly criticizing and berating Gavin for his shortcomings.

He stopped pacing and stared out the window at the scraggly lawn. The gardens were tired as well, nodding blooms fighting for supremacy

A Lesson in Love

among the weeds. Just like England against the Nazis. Tired and a bit bedraggled, but still doing her best to beat back the evil that threatened to overtake her. A woman in overalls appeared, pushing a reel mower. Her hair was covered with a kerchief, and she was either singing or talking to herself: another woman picking up the void of some man who'd gone into combat. She marched forward and back, cutting swaths of grass.

Rather than be caught staring, he moved away from the window and leaned against the wall, his arms wrapped around his middle. Another glance at the clock. Three more minutes had elapsed. He rubbed his forehead, then whipped up his head at the sound of footsteps. Too heavy to be Isobel's but maybe some nurse with news.

A man of perhaps seventy, clutching a bowler in his hands, was led into the room by a nurse he'd never seen before. She murmured something to him, and he nodded before finding his way to one of the wooden Windsor chairs. The nurse exited, and the man sent Gavin a curt nod, lines of worry etched on his face. Bowing his head, the man sighed. What tragedy had befallen his family? Gavin turned away. *Please, Lord, grant him Your peace and heal his loved one.*

More footsteps, and Gavin's gut tightened, but the sound faded a moment later. He huffed out a sigh. Stillwater hadn't commented at first when Gavin indicated he needed him to cover for one more day while he retrieved Isobel from the hospital, but the man's smirk had said volumes. Making no secret of his ambitions, he probably didn't care why he would remain in charge, as long as it happened. He'd received Gavin's thanks as the king might from one of his subjects, and told Gavin to take as long as he needed, acting as if he had the authority to grant the time.

When they returned to the manor, she'd be under the care of her friends. She wouldn't need him to keep her company, reading aloud, or discussing theories about education. Back at the helm, he'd run the school, writing the endless reports for the Ministry of Education, and holding classes for the lads. She'd recover and eventually go back to the fields. He'd miss their time together more than he wanted to admit. Firm, but caring, she'd forced him to confront the complicated relationship with his father. Her words had been a balm to his ravaged soul, and he'd felt lighter than he had in decades. The desire to sweep her into his arms and kiss her had been overwhelming, but he'd refrained. He'd give her a proper kiss when the time was right, and definitely not out of gratitude. Not that—

"Mr. Emerson?"

He whirled. Lost in thought, he hadn't heard the nurse's approach.

"Miss Turvine is waiting for you in the lobby."

"Excellent. Thank you." He sprinted to the doorway, then halted, and turned around. "And thank you for all you and the staff have done to ensure Miss Turvine's recovery."

She dipped her head. "Of course, sir."

Gavin rushed down the corridor and burst into the lobby.

Isobel looked up, a wan smile on her face. "Thanks for helping me break out of this joint," she said in a raspy Jimmy Cagneyesque accent.

He chuckled. "Someone is feeling better, although you do look a bit peaked. We'll get you home as soon as possible. I'll go retrieve the getaway car."

Her laughter followed him out the door, and he grinned as he trotted toward the Bentley the earl insisted he use because "Nothing was too good for our Miss Turvine." Gavin wasn't the only one enamored with the woman. Two minutes later, he guided the vehicle to the entrance and jumped out, skirted the back of the car, and opened the passenger door. Still in the wheelchair, Isobel waited outside, chatting with the nurse. He approached and crooked his arm. "Your chariot awaits, madam."

"Thank you, kind sir." Despite her obvious fatigue, Isobel's eyes twinkled as she slipped her hand into his elbow. "I'm ready to return to the castle."

The warmth of her fingers sent tingles to his shoulder, but he schooled his features, or so he hoped. As he helped her into the car, he caught the fresh scent of her hair, and he stifled the urge to inhale deeply. Before he could do something he regretted, he tucked the blanket around her that Tracey had pressed into his hands last night, when he'd stopped by the cottage to let the girls know of Isobel's release. They'd cheered, even the two who regularly bickered for no other reason than they seemed to enjoy the sparring. As he bid them good night, he could hear the discussions about what they would do to welcome her home. It seemed she couldn't ask for better colleagues and friends.

Sliding behind the wheel, he glanced at her. "Ready?"

"Ready."

He pulled away from the curb. "Lie your head back and rest. I'll have us at Kingsley Manor in short order."

"I've done nothing but rest. I'm fine." She shrugged. "And the doctor says I can't go back to work for another week, so I'll have plenty of time as a layabout. Tell me about the boys. How are they doing?"

"Good. The incident was a life lesson, so they are a bit somber, mulling over all that happened, but we're not letting them wallow in it. We shortened classes and gave them more time outside."

"The challenge is balance, isn't it? They must learn from their mistakes, but if we're too heavy-handed, we can do damage."

"As I'm well-aware, but thanks to you, I'm on the mend." Gavin forced a smile. "In celebration of your homecoming, the boys have prepared lunch, so I hope you're hungry."

Isobel rubbed her stomach. "Famished. What's on the menu?"

"Nothing fancy, just ham sandwiches and potato salad."

"Potatoes."

He chuckled. "Seen enough tubers for one lifetime?"

"You might say that." Her laugh ended in a cough. "Ouch."

"Enough talking. Your doctor will skin me alive if you regress." He turned into the lane that led to the manor. "In all seriousness, are you worn out? Would you like to eat in your room? I can have your food delivered."

She shook her head. "I want to be part of the festivities." She straightened and glanced out the window. "Is that the boys? What are they doing?"

"Greeting their favorite person." He grinned and resisted the urge to lace his fingers with hers. Instead, he tightened his grip on the wheel, guided the car into the large graveled expanse in front of the manor, then swung the vehicle around so the lads were on her side. As he came to a stop, two of the students unfurled a sheet on which had been painted the words "Welcome Home Miss Turvine."

Isobel pressed her hands against her chest, and her eyes shimmered with wetness as her chin trembled. Her gaze bounced between the boys and Gavin. "Are you responsible for this?"

"All their idea. Now, wait there, and I'll help you out."

Nodding, she turned back to the window and waved.

Cheering, the boys returned the gesture and called out as Gavin jumped from the car and hurried to open her door. He crooked his elbow, bracing himself for the zing of electricity that would surely accompany her hand on his arm. As they walked toward the young men and teachers, she leaned heavily on him, attesting to her weariness. He would not be so bold as to carry her into the dining room, but the temptation was great. "Well done, lads. I know you have a speech prepared, but Miss Turvine is somewhat tired, so let's get her settled inside first. And she must save her voice, so don't pummel her with questions. You boys go on ahead, and we'll take up the rear."

As one, the students broke into a run and hurried through the massive doors, their laughter and conversation echoing off the stone. The instructors followed at a more stately pace. Isobel sent him a dazzling smile, and his knees nearly buckled. There was no longer any doubt. He'd fallen for this woman, but little did she know she held his heart in her hands. Dare he tell her?

A Lesson in Love

Chapter Twenty

Seated at the ten-foot gleaming cherrywood Queen Anne-style table, Isobel sagged against the back of the chair. Loathe to admit it, she was worn out after the ride from the hospital, but her heart was full. According to Margery, the earl had insisted on the use of the china that bore his family crest. Silverware, crystal glasses, and linen napkins completed the ensemble as if he were entertaining a fellow member of the peerage rather than a passel of schoolboys and a troupe of Land Girls. On her right, he looked like a child at Christmastime, his face wreathed in smiles. On her left, Gavin sat with his arm across the back of her chair, the tangy scent of his aftershave hovering between them.

The boys delivered platters piled with ham sandwiches, and Cook and two of the teachers followed with tureens of tomato soup. Isobel's stomach rumbled from the aromas as the students lined up in front of the table, their hair slicked back and wearing their best clothes.

Harry stepped forward, handed her a vase filled with wildflowers, then cleared his throat. "I want you to know how sorry I am for you getting hurt. It was stupid of me to sneak into the barn for a smoke, and I'm never going to do anything like that again." He peeked at the earl, who gave him an encouraging smile. "I've been working with Lord Flagler to make amends, and I'm grateful he didn't toss me out. Thank you, sir."

The earl dipped his head in acknowledgment, then motioned for Harry to continue at the same time one of the younger boys jabbed him with an elbow. Isobel swallowed a smile but exchanged an amused glance with Gavin.

A quick, dark look from Harry, then his features cleared as he shrugged. "Anyway, we all want to say how much we missed you. It's not been the same. We've learnt lots about farming from you, but mostly how to be an upright person no matter what's going on. As part of our way to say thanks, we put together a schedule to help with the work, in addition to our studies. Mr. Emerson and Mr. Stillwater have approved it, so you just need to say the word."

"Thank you for your apology, Harry. I accept, but as far as helping with our tasks, your schoolwork comes first."

"Yes, ma'am." Harry nodded. "But Mr. Balfour says that farm kids do their chores before breakfast, so we'll just have to get up earlier."

Isobel turned and gaped at Gavin. "Was this your idea?"

"Not at all. The boys came to me of their own volition."

Tears welled in her eyes, and she blinked away the moisture. "This is a lot to take in, Harry, and I appreciate your offer. It speaks volumes to how you and the others have matured in the last few days. I am very proud of all of you. Let me speak to the other girls, and I will get back to you."

"Thank you, Miss Turvine." Harry looked left, then right, and the boys bowed in unison before breaking rank and heading to the round tables set around the room.

Gavin ladled soup into her bowl, then using a pair of tongs, put a half sandwich onto her plate. As he returned to the platter for another half, she shook her head, so he put the food on his own plate. "You're exhausted, aren't you?"

"Yes, but you…the boys… This is worth it. I can sleep later." She gave him a wan smile. "I'm probably going to need a lift to the cottage."

"The lads tried to make arrangements with the earl for you to have a room in the main house until you're released to full duty, but the girls wanted to take care of you." He picked up his spoon. "Do you see the impact you've had on these young people's lives, the students and your girls? One of the many reasons I love you. Now, eat up."

Her jaw hung slack, and she snapped it closed before she could be caught staring. With trembling fingers, she picked up her spoon and scooped up some of the steaming liquid. He loved her? Certainly not. Surely, he was just using the expression in a casual manner. He couldn't possibly love her, not like a man cares for a woman.

"Cook has outdone herself with the soup, don't you think?" Gavin slurped another spoonful. "This takes me back to my childhood. Tomato soup was one of Mum's favorites."

"Ah, yes, delicious."

"How would you know?" He gestured toward the utensil gripped in her hand. "You've haven't taken a bite yet."

"Good grief." Her face heated, and she sipped from her spoon. Flavor exploded on her tongue, and the warm soup soothed her throat. "Mmm. You're right. It's wonderful."

"Your face is flushed." He looked at her, a crease in his forehead. "You've overdone, so finish your meal, and we'll get you upstairs where you can rest."

"I am starting to fold, but the boys went to a lot of work, and I'm hungry. I'll be all right."

"Are you sure?"

"Yes, I won't take much longer to eat, then Margery can help me upstairs." Isobel grinned. "She'll want to see my new digs, so she can tell the girls all about them."

Gavin chuckled. "I'm sure, and you'll be able to sleep through the night without nurses waking you for medication or to ask how you're doing."

She giggled, and they ate in companionable silence. The food filled her stomach, and tension slipped from her shoulders. Her eyelids fluttered as she pushed away her empty dishware. Covering her mouth, she yawned. She was tired enough to fall asleep sitting up in the chair. That's why she read more into Gavin's statement about love than she should. Weariness was addling her brain and her emotions. A good night's sleep would put everything back into perspective. Dinner suddenly sat like a stone in her stomach. She didn't want perspective; she wanted more than friendship with this dear, sweet man, but it could never be.

Tossing his napkin on the table next to his plate, Gavin sent a surreptitious glance at Isobel. Despite the smile on her face, her skin had taken on an ashen cast, and she slumped against the back of the chair. His heart clenched. "Time to get you to…the cottage." Polite people didn't discuss bed. He pushed back his chair, then caught Margery's eye and motioned to Isobel. Her friend jumped up, said something to the others at her table, then hurried toward them. She skirted the table to stand next to Isobel. "No offense, but you looked bushed, and frankly I'm ready to be kid free. The car is waiting out front."

With a quiet sigh, Isobel nodded and struggled to her feet.

Gavin wrapped his arm around her waist to steady her, her lithe form fitting to his as if they were two pieces of the same puzzle. He ignored Margery's knowing smirk. "Let me help you to the car."

"Thank you." Her words were breathy and barely above a whisper.

"Would you rather take my arm? I, um, that is—"

"This is perfect. If you release me, I can't guarantee I won't fall onto the floor in a heap." A small smile curved one corner of her mouth. "So, if Margery will lead the way instead of gawking at us, we can get to it."

Gavin chuckled as Margery sputtered, then shrugged and made her way through the tables to the door at the far end of the room. Senses reeling at the feel of Isobel's hip under his hand, he gulped. He was enjoying the situation way too much. He guided her to the exit, and her steps seemed to stutter the farther they walked. "I should have been more mindful of your fatigue."

"It crept up on me. Don't blame yourself. You've been a brick through all of this. I'm not sure what I'd have done without you."

Warmth spread through his limbs, and he shrugged. "The girls would have managed."

"But it wouldn't be nearly as fun."

They made it to the front door where Margery sat behind the wheel of the earl's car, the passenger door open and waiting. Isobel gripped the frame, then lowered herself onto the leather seat with a grunt. "Home, James. And don't spare the horses."

Gavin grinned as he tucked Isobel's skirt around her, then closed the door. Even in her weakness, she hadn't lost her sense of humor. He banged on the roof of the vehicle, then waved. The engine purred as the car rolled away. He watched the taillights fade in the growing darkness.

"How're you holding up, old man?"

Nearly jumping out of his skin, Gavin whirled, his hand pressed against his thundering heart. "Pretty well, considering you almost gave me a stroke. Don't sneak up on me."

Alastair thumped him on the back. "Hardly. You were so mesmerized by a certain young lady you didn't hear my approach." He shoved his hands into his pockets. "Are you coming back inside?"

"If you and the others can handle cleanup, I've got paperwork to complete."

"Paperwork, right. Sounds a bit woolly." Alastair turned on his heel, then glanced over his shoulder. "Anytime you'd like to talk, my ear is available."

Gavin didn't bother responding that there was nothing to discuss because they'd both know he'd be lying. His history with Alastair went back decades, and the two could finish each other's sentences. The man was his best friend, and who better to share his conflicted feelings with, but not tonight. "Another time."

With a wave, Alastair sauntered toward the manor whistling Vera Lynn's "We'll Meet Again" as he went.

Rolling his eyes at Alastair's musical message, Gavin set off in the opposite direction. Yes, he had reports to complete, but he doubted he could focus on the mundane task. A chilly breeze brushed his cheeks, and he lifted his face to the sky, the gibbous moon casting an eerie light across the grassy expanse. Before he talked to his friend, he'd spend some time with God.

With a sigh, Gavin strolled toward the gardens on the west side of the mansion. Moonlight guided his steps, the ground soft beneath his feet. He followed the stone path that curved between the shrubs until he found the bench nestled among a copse of trees. Another sigh, and he dropped onto the wooden slats. Leaning forward, he propped his arms on his thighs and bowed his head.

"Forgive me, Father. This is long overdue. Help me know what you want of me. I'm a tangled mess. You heard my oath all those years ago to never marry, and it felt right. But now…" He scrubbed at his face with cold fingers. "Now, it feels like a foolish vow made by a child. You heard me tonight. I told her I loved her, yet she didn't seem to notice. Is that a blessing? Is that Your way of telling me this thing…these feelings…aren't meant to go anywhere? What do I do? Would You have me fall in love with her only to go our separate ways at the end of it all? I've been avoiding the truth, but then I thought I was going to lose her in the fire, and life didn't seem worth living without her. Should I tell her? What if she doesn't feel the same? Lead me, Father. Please, lead me."

Gavin fell silent, listening, ears straining for words from his Lord. Nothing. No feelings of peace or contentment. In the past, it only meant one thing. Wait. He'd learned the hard way not to plow ahead of God, but that didn't mean he had to like it.

Chapter Twenty-One

With a sigh, Isobel sat up on the bed and rearranged the pillows. She'd been wrestling with the covers for the last few minutes. She flopped against on the cushions and stared out the window. Truth be told, it was her attitude that needed adjusting rather than the bedclothes. She was sick to death of lying around, watching the girls work in the distant fields visible through the glass.

Four days had passed since her return to the manor, and her throat was more dry than sore. She was no longer exhausted after each trip to the bathroom, and she'd slept more hours than been awake. But the doctor had said a week, and the girls wouldn't budge on their refusal to let her do anything. She'd scream if it wouldn't damage the progress she'd made in her recovery.

Her gaze strayed to the stack of books on the nightstand, two Agatha Christie mysteries, *Pride and Prejudice*, *Gone with the Wind*, and James Hilton's *Random Harvest*. The girl who'd lent her the book gushed on about the upcoming film of Hilton's novel and that the dreamy Ronald Colman would play the lead. Isobel was more of a Cary Grant fan herself, but theaters were few and far between in Yorkshire. None, was more like it.

Another sigh escaped, and she shoved the pile to one side which revealed her Bible. Her stomach tightened. Wallowing in self-pity, she hadn't opened the leather-bound volume since yesterday. She swallowed the lump that formed in her throat. If she'd lost herself in the Book's pages, she'd be in a much better frame of mind. "Forgive me, Lord."

She reached for the Bible, and her fingers curled around the thin, supple volume. She held it to her chest for a long moment, then laid it on her lap and began to thumb through the tissue-like pages. Arriving at the Psalms, she flipped through, reading snippets.

Landing on the 139th chapter, she mouthed the words, their archaic rhythm somehow soothing, "O Lord, Thou hast searched me, and known me. Thou knowest my downsitting and mine uprising, Thou understandest my thought afar off. Thou compassest my path and my lying down, and art acquainted with all my ways. For there is not a word in my tongue, but, lo, O Lord, Thou knowest it altogether. Thou hast beset me behind and before, and laid Thine hand upon me. Such knowledge is too wonderful for me; it is high, I cannot attain unto it. Whither shall I go from Thy spirit? Or whither shall I flee from Thy presence?"

Such flowery language. A king with the heart of a poet, Israel's leader, David, had captured the highs and lows of life. She stroked the pages and closed her eyes. "Father, thank You for the words of Your servant, David, and the reminder that You are with me, no matter what. That You knew what was going to happen to me. You saved my life, and I'm so grateful, yet here I am moaning about being trapped in bed. Hardly the worst of times. Instead, I should be using the time to commune with

You. Strengthen my faith, and show me Your plans for me. Help me to savor each moment of my life, no matter what is happening."

Tears seeped from the corners of her eyes as warmth enveloped her. Warmth that had nothing to do with the covers she was buried under. "Thank You, Father."

Footsteps sounded in the hallway, and she swiped at the moisture on her cheeks, then scooted higher in the bed. The treads faded, and her shoulders slumped. Of course, whoever it was passed by. There was work to be done. No time for visiting until the sun went down.

Enough lollygagging. Isobel laid her Bible on the bedside table, then flung back the covers. She padded across the gorgeous mauve, tan, and blue rug: Persian, no doubt, and picked up the Royal Doulton pitcher and poured water into the ewer. Using the plush cloth on the dresser, she washed her face, then stripped her nightgown and gave herself a sponge bath before toweling off with another luxurious cloth. She'd been treated like a queen these last days.

The clothes she'd been wearing the night of the fire lay washed and folded on the Queen Anne chair. She quickly donned the garments, then grinned at herself in the mirror. Fully bathed and dressed, and she didn't need a nap from the exertion.

More footsteps—those of at least two people—as she brushed her hair, then plaited it in a single braid down her back. Finished with her preparations, she turned and headed for the door. She couldn't remain in the room one more minute. As she reached for the knob, the rumbling tones of Gavin's voice reached her ears. Then a woman's. Margery? Isobel strained to hear their words.

"….need to tell her," said the woman.

"I… You don't know…talking about."

Isobel put her ear close to the crack where the door met the frame. Who were they discussing?

"You're reading too much into the situation," Gavin said.

"Hardly. I see the way you look at her, especially when you think no one is looking. You've got it bad, Gavin, and you're going to lose her if you don't declare yourself."

"And what if she turns me down?" Anguish colored his words.

"Not likely. Isobel's just as besotted, and the two of you are the only ones around here who don't recognize it."

Isobel clamped her hand over her mouth. He had feelings for her? Margery knew about her feelings for him? She'd barely admitted them to herself.

"It's too late," Gavin scoffed. "I'm too old."

"Age is irrelevant." Margery huffed out a loud sigh. "Not that it's any of your business, but maybe my story will knock some sense into you. Ten years ago, I was walking out with someone. He was nearly twenty years my senior, but that didn't matter to me. He treated me like a queen, and we were good together, complemented each other's strengths and weaknesses, you know? Then my so-called friends started questioning how I could love someone so *old*." She spat out the word.

"They kept at me until I became embarrassed to be seen with him, and told him we were through." Her voice faltered. "I broke his heart. And mine. A month later, I realized what a fool I'd been and tried to find him. He was gone, left the city without telling a soul where he was going, and I lost my chance for something wonderful. A day doesn't go by that I don't regret my stupidity. I would give anything for just one more day with him. Don't be me. Learn from my mistake."

"Thanks for sharing your loss. You can trust me not to tell anyone." Compassion warmed his voice. "But how can you be sure she—"

"Because I know Isobel. She doesn't easily allow people in, especially men, but with you… Trust me. She cares for you. A lot." She cleared her throat. "But you better not hurt her or you'll answer to me. And that won't be pretty. Understood?"

Silence. Then footsteps again. They moved past her door, then faded.

Isobel's pulse raced as she rested her forehead on the door. Had he shrugged? Nodded? Frowned? Why hadn't he said anything? Should she find Margery and tell her she'd overheard everything? How could she look either of them in the eye? Especially Gavin. How could she be around him and act like nothing had happened? What if he did care for her, maybe even love her, but not enough to pursue something permanent? What if he did? She caught her lower lip in her teeth. Life was so much easier when she was teaching seven-year-olds.

She straightened, then squared her shoulders. Hiding out in her room, she was acting like one of her students. Yet, she would have told them to face their fears head-on, with prayer. She bowed her head. "All right, Lord, I'm laying this at Your feet. I'm a mess after what I heard. I do love him. There, I've said it. But, please protect my heart because I'm terrified."

I'm with you, My child.

Tears prickled the backs of her eyes, and she whispered, "Thank You." For a long moment, she remained in place, letting God's love wash over her, then a noise sounded from below, and she raised her head. She grabbed the knob. "Here we go into the fray."

Chapter Twenty-Two

Rubbing at the puckered scar tissue on his arm, Gavin gazed out the window at the cloudless blue sky. At its zenith, the sun shone with unseasonable brightness, lighting up the vast fields where the women were sowing winter wheat. The dark-brown soil seemed to shimmer. Rays poured through the glass panes and pooled on the floor, heating the room. Aromas of chalk dust and floor wax filled his nostrils.

The sound of pencils scratching across the boys' papers mingled with the occasional sigh or murmur as they worked on their exams. His vision strayed to his pocket watch that he'd laid on the desk. "Ten more minutes, lads."

A groan swept through the group, and he refrained from commenting. Unless he was mistaken, all would do well on the test. With Isobel discharged from the hospital, worry lines had disappeared from the boys' faces. He'd hated to see their concern, and despite his assurances she was fine and would make a full recovery, according to the doctor, they hadn't truly relaxed until she'd returned to the manor. It was bad enough the poor souls' lives had been uprooted by a war they barely understood, but they'd obviously grown to love her, so their angst ran deep.

In the few minutes left of the class period, he studied the three boys he thought of as the three musketeers. Henry: hunched over the desk with his forehead wrinkled so deeply his eyebrows met above his nose. Calvin: chin propped in one hand, his tongue poking out one side of his mouth. He'd apparently run his fingers across his scalp because his blond hair spiked in several places. Iain: The more somber of the three of them, he pursed his lips for a moment, shook his head, then laid down his pencil. Typical that he'd completed the exam before the others. His mind was razor-sharp, and he rarely let himself get distracted.

Voices and footfalls filtered through the closed door from the corridor, and Gavin checked his watch. "Time's up. Please pass your papers forward, then remain in your seats for a moment."

Papers rustled as several of the students blew out their breath in loud sighs. Shoes scuffled on the floor, and books thudded onto the desks. Gavin swallowed a grin. Decades had passed since he was a student, but he still remembered the mixed feelings of relief and doubt after exams. A dozen expectant faces turned toward him as he collected the stacks of papers from the first student in each row. He laid them on the desk, then leaned against the mammoth centuries-old piece of furniture, and crossed his arms. "I don't know about you, lads, but I could use a bit of a break. We've worked hard this term, and my brain is about used up. I say, would you have any objections to taking a headmaster's holiday?"

Cheering, the boys exchanged looks of delight. As the sound died down, Harry raised one hand. "What about the other students, sir? They've worked hard, too. Wouldn't be fair for just one class to receive the holiday."

"Quite right, Mr. Kemp." Gavin beamed at Harry who was maturing more and more each day. "I'll issue a proclamation at dinner tonight for the morrow. How's that sound?"

"Tickety-boo," yelled Peter Donovan, and laughter followed.

Harry chuckled and shrugged. "Couldn't have said it better myself."

Gavin rubbed his palms together. "That settles it. Meanwhile, we don't have many of these balmy days remaining, so I believe a game of cricket is in order. Change your clothes and meet me on the south lawn in thirty minutes."

Conversation buzzed as the boys rose and hurried from the room, their voices fading quickly. Gavin shoved his hands into his pockets and cast another glance out the window. Movement caught his eye. Isobel. The familiar flutter filled his stomach as if a chipmunk was trapped inside. Three days had passed since his whispered conversation with Margery in the hallway outside Isobel's room. Three days of wrestling with himself about approaching her while she was recovering. Two nights of praying. God had finally given him peace about the situation, but daylight would come, and fear would creep back into his heart. What if she said no? She wouldn't laugh at him, but the rejection would hurt all the same.

"Quite a view from up here, old chap."

Pivoting, Gavin frowned at Alastair. "Don't sneak up on me."

"Hardly, and you keep saying that, but your engrossment in a certain beautiful woman outside prevents you from hearing me approach." Alastair smirked, then clapped Gavin on the back. "I hear there is a cricket match on the schedule. A great excuse for you to rest your weary bones next to her and watch us youngsters play."

"Ha. You're only five years younger than me."

"But I'm not looking for an excuse to spend time with the lovely Miss Turvine. When are you going to ask for her hand?"

Gavin huffed out a sigh and shouldered past his friend. "Time's wasting. I told the lads to meet me on the field in thirty minutes."

"Then we can talk as we walk." Alastair grinned as he caught up with him. They stepped into the corridor and began the trek to the front door. "I know you're not one to discuss your feelings, but it's obvious you care about this woman. A great deal. And you're miserable wondering if she feels the same. As terrifying as the prospect of asking is, you've got to fish or cut bait."

"Fish or cut bait?" Gavin rolled his eyes. "Aren't you the romantic."

Alastair shrugged. "Probably why I'm still single."

"Sorr—"

"Forget it. I'm happier this way. And don't change the subject." They reached the immense foyer, and Alastair laid his hand on Gavin's arm. "I'm serious, old man. Don't let her get away. With all the chaos in this place, there will never be a good time to ask her, so I suggest you take care of this today. I'll handle the game, and you propose."

"Have I told you what a good friend you are?"

Alastair's face held an expression of mock disappointment. "Not often enough."

Gavin snorted a laugh and shook off his friend's hand. "I'll try to remedy that. Meanwhile, let's get on with this before I lose my nerve. This is nearly as terrifying as facing the Huns all those years ago." He took a deep breath, yanked open the door, and strode toward the grassy lawn where the boys had begun to congregate. "Once more into the breach!"

"The Bard, eh? Good choice."

As they hurried toward the commotion, Isobel rose from her chair and raised her hand in greeting. Her face glowed as she sent him a broad smile. His pulse tripped, and he glanced at Alastair. His friend didn't comment, but his wiggling eyebrows said volumes.

"Miss Turvine, you are looking much improved." Alastair bowed. "I'm pleased to see you outside enjoying the day. We have few of these left."

"Thank you, Mr. Balfour." Her cheeks were flushed. "I'm allowed to return to the fields in two days, and I'm more than ready. There are only so many books to read or records to listen to. Despite the size of the manor, I'm suffering from a bit of cabin fever."

"Then watching the boys play is just the thing." He jabbed Gavin with an elbow. "This old man will slow us down, so he's agreed to stay off the field. Do you mind some company?"

"Of course not." She tapped her chin with an index finger and shot them a wicked smile. "Although, I'd wager he's not the detriment you think."

Gavin gaped at her as Alastair guffawed. The pink on her face deepened to red, and she dropped her eyes, cheeky attitude gone.

"And with that, Miss Turvine, I'll leave you to it." Alastair trotted toward the boys. "All right, gents, let's show Miss Turvine what we've got."

"I, um, guess that's the cue to take our seats." Heart pounding, Gavin waited until she sat, then he dropped to one knee. It was now or never.

Chapter Twenty-Three

Heart thundering in her ears, Isobel stared at Gavin whose face held a mixture of apprehension and admiration. No, more than admiration. Dare she think it was love? He was on one knee. That could only mean one thing, couldn't it? Tears welled in her eyes, and she pressed her lips together to keep them from trembling.

She laced her fingers together as he cleared his throat. Then cleared it again. Had she read him wrong? Was he dreading the words? Had he discovered something terrible and needed to break the news to her gently? Her stomach churned. She could wait no longer. "What—"

"Isobel."

"What is it? You're frightening me."

"I'm making a right mess of this." Gavin sighed, then took one of her hands in his, cradling them in his warm palms. "There's nothing wrong. In fact, I'm hoping it's about to get better." He swallowed, then licked his lips. "I haven't been this nervous since... Actually, I'm not sure I've ever been this nervous. Anyway, um, I care about you, more than I've ever cared about another woman. No, that's not right. What I mean to say is I love you."

Isobel gasped. "Gavin—"

"Please let me finish. If I don't, I might not get through it." He sent her a wry smile. "I've never met anyone like you. You're smart and clever and witty. Creative, too. And gracious. Your quiet faith has made me examine my own. And you're beautiful." He stroked her jaw with his thumb. "So very beautiful. You make me want to be a better man, a man you deserve. I'm older than you by a good bit, and I'm not one hundred percent…my arm, you know, but I couldn't go any longer without declaring myself, not after almost losing you in the fire. I had to—have to—tell you how much I love you and that I want nothing more than to spend the rest of our lives showing you just how much. Isobel Turvine, will you do me the honor of being my wife?"

"Oh, Gavin." Isobel's words came out as a whisper, and a single tear tumbled from her eye. He loved her. He wanted to marry her. How was that possible? She was thirty-five years old. A spinster. Yet, he said all those lovely things about her, and he thought she was beautiful. Even with the lines on her face from spending hours in the field. And just the other day, she'd found a gray hair. How long before they took over the black?

His eyebrows came together, and his smile faltered. "Now, you're frightening me. It seems you want to let me down easily. That you don't feel the same." He dropped her hand as if burned. "I'm sorry. I—"

She put her index finger against his lips for a second, then withdrew, her skin tingling where she'd touched him. "It's me who is sorry. I was so overwhelmed, so amazed that you could possibly love me that I couldn't respond. I love you, too. I wasn't looking for a relationship, and at my age never dreamed I would find one. I would be thrilled to marry you, Gavin Emerson."

"You have made me the happiest man on earth." Gray eyes sparkling, he cupped her face in his hands, then lowered his mouth on hers. Gentle, but firm, then the kiss deepened, and she lost herself in the moment.

Cheering sounded, and they broke apart as the boys charged toward them, Alastair bringing up the rear and wearing a broad grin. He winked at Gavin, then turned to Isobel. "Did you agree to marry this old man, Miss Turvine?"

Gavin wrapped one arm around her shoulder, and she snuggled against him. "As a matter of fact, I did, Mr. Balfour, but I wouldn't call him old. He's…seasoned."

Alastair threw his head back and laughed as the boys encircled the pair.

"Congratulations, Miss Turvine, Mr. Emerson."

"Does that mean you won't be a Land Girl anymore?"

"When are you going to get married?"

"Where are you going to get married?"

"Who will be your best man, Mr. Emerson?"

Gavin released her and climbed to his feet, holding up his hands as if in surrender. "Enough questions, lads. We appreciate your excitement and good wishes, but we've only just agreed to marry, so the logistics are hardly worked out, are they?" His gaze bounced to Alastair. "So much for keeping this between us."

"That's not what happened." Alastair ruffled Harry's hair. "This one saw you kissing and wondered if you'd finally popped the question. You see, I'm not the only one around here who recognized what the two of you feel for each other."

Isobel's face warmed. She'd thought she'd been so discreet with her emotions. Margery would get a kick out of the situation. Margery! She raised her head and looked toward the fields where the girls were working. Would her friend be angry that the boys knew about Gavin's marriage proposal before her? Doubtful, but Isobel would make sure she heard before the rest of the Land Girls.

"I've embarrassed you, Miss Turvine. Please accept my apologies."

"You've nothing to be sorry for, Mr. Balfour. After being a teacher all these years, I should have the constitution of a rhinoceros."

He chuckled. "Perhaps, but primary students are different than these louts, who should head back to the cricket field and give you some privacy." He clapped his hands. "Come, lads, the excitement's over."

"Bye, Miss Turvine." Jostling each other, the boys broke into a run. Alastair put two fingers to his forehead in a salute, then turned on his heel, and strolled to the students.

Isobel smiled at Gavin as he lowered himself back to the ground, then reached up to lace his fingers with hers. His gaze caressed her face. "Well, that was a bit much. Are you all right?"

"Absolutely. The boys mean a lot to me. They've become an extended family."

"I'm glad you feel that way because despite the Allied victories, we've surely got another three or four years to this war, and they're here for the duration." He tilted his head. "Which brings us to the point of deciding when to marry. Frankly, at my age, I don't want to wait until after the war, but I want to respect you. Do you feel the need for a long engagement?"

She squeezed his hand. Such a gentleman. "Hardly. At *my* age, I don't want to wait either. I'd like the girls to be there, and most will leave in January. We won't need them all to manage the hydroponics."

"How about a Christmas wedding? Can you pull things together in a few weeks? I don't want to rush you."

"With all these gals?" She tittered. "We can whip a wedding together in no time. Besides, I don't need anything extravagant. Just you, a minister, and my friends."

Gavin chuckled. "The earl will want to do a bit more than that. Quite a coup, getting married in a manor home. You realize with my salary we won't be living like this after the war."

She gaped at him in exaggerated shock and pressed her hand against her throat. "What? No mansion? No castle? Another dream shattered. I may have to change my answer."

His eyebrow shot up. "Aren't you the sassy one?"

"Just keeping you on your toes, my love." Laughing she poked his shoulder. "But in all seriousness, a flat in London or a shack in Yorkshire makes no difference to me. When you have love you're rich enough. Now, kiss me again. We have to make up for lost time."

A Lesson in Love

December 26, 1942: Boxing Day

Epilogue

Candlelight flickered and cast reflections against the windowpanes as Gavin rubbed the scar tissue on his arm and rocked on his heels in the great hall, waiting for Isobel to appear in the doorway. If he'd had his way, the wedding would have occurred after breakfast instead of the night wedding Isobel wanted. The day had dragged with each minute, inching forward like a snail. His stomach quivered as if a pair of squirrels were running amok, and perspiration trickled in between his shoulder blades and dampened his palms.

Pine garlands hung from the windowsills, and the ten-foot spruce Christmas tree stood sentry in the corner, festooned with ribbons and antique ornaments the earl had dragged down from the attic. Yesterday's festivities had been reminiscent of his own childhood Christmases with presents and stockings and a meal fit for royalty. The Red Cross had delivered items for the boys earlier in the week, including poppers which were deployed within minutes. Giggles and shrieks had filled every corner of the manor home, the lads managing to forget their homesickness and sadness about the world at war.

The trio of musicians played softly, their stringed instruments filling the room with dulcet tones. What he knew about classical music wouldn't fill a paragraph, so he had no idea whose music entertained them, other than the composer was not German. No law or official ban was in place, but most people agreed it was bad form to listen to German songs. A shame, considering the beauty of their work.

His gaze strayed to the guests, mostly strangers, seated in the hodgepodge collection of chairs gathered from all over the house. The earl had issued an announcement in the nearby town about the wedding, and residents had come out in full force, bringing gifts and good wishes. Dressed in their best clothing and hair combed, the boys filled the first four rows. They fidgeted and whispered among themselves, but he couldn't blame them. He caught Harry's eye, and the boy grinned, sending him an imperceptible nod.

Gavin's chest swelled as he returned the lad's smile. It was inappropriate to have favorites among his students, but the young man had taken up a corner of his heart like none of the others. He'd matured since the fire, maintaining his wit, but channeling it into entertaining and uplifting acts rather than pranks. The boy was sharp as a whip and had begun to apply himself, quickly rising to the top of every subject. He'd go far in whatever area of study he chose.

"Stop twitching, old man." Alastair nudged him. "She'll be here."

"This has been the longest day of my life." Gavin spoke out of the corner of his mouth. "I'd have settled for two witnesses at the register office."

"Buck up. It will all be over soon. Well, soon enough. You've got dinner and dancing. Don't you want to dance with your wife?"

A sigh escaped. "Yes, and years from now I'll enjoy memories of this special day, but for now…" He shrugged and went back to studying the room. Seconds later, Isobel appeared in the doorway, a vision in white froth. A veil covered her face, and the simple Grecian-style gown clung to her lithe figure. Apparently, the girls had pooled their resources to get a dress made for their friend.

The violins ceased playing, leaving the cello to continue its dulcet rendition of Pachelbel's Canon in D. Even a war couldn't stand up against the traditional bridal march. Rustling sounded as members of the congregation rose to their feet, and Isobel glided down the aisle on the earl's arm. Gavin stifled the urge to sprint toward her instead sending her a dazzling smile that he hoped convey the overwhelming love that filled his heart.

Finally, she arrived by his side, and the earl pulled back her veil, then transferred her hand to Gavin's. Her fingers were cold, and he squeezed them gently. He wasn't alone in his nervousness. He would never be alone as long as he lived. They would partner through whatever time remained on earth.

With God's help, he'd set aside the last vestiges of bitterness and anger toward his father. Gavin would never understand his father's need to belittle him, but he could choose to forgive the man and vow to live a different life, to encourage and exhort those around him. His injuries and flaws didn't define him; his adoption as a child of God did, and he would do his best to exude that every day as he walked beside his treasure of a wife. He turned his head and winked, bringing a pink tinge to Isobel's cheeks. She winked in return. Life would be an adventure with her, and he couldn't wait to get started.

The End

What did you think of *A Lesson in Love*?

Thank you so much for purchasing *A Lesson in Love*. You could have selected any number of books to read, but you chose this book.

I hope it added encouragement and exhortation to your life. If so, it would be nice if you could share this book with your family and friends by posting to one or more of your favorite social media outlets.

If you enjoyed this book and found some benefit in reading it, I'd appreciate it if you could take some time to post a review on Amazon, Kobo, BN, Goodreads, BookBub or other book review site of your choice. Your feedback and support will help me to improve my writing craft for future projects and make this book even better.

Thank you again for your purchase.

Blessings,
Linda Shenton Matchett

A Lesson in Love

Acknowledgments

Although writing a book is a solitary task, it is not a solitary journey. There have been many who have helped and encouraged me along the way.

My parents, Richard and Jean Shenton, who presented me with my first writing tablet and encouraged me to capture my imagination with words. Thanks, Mom and Dad!

Scribes212 – my ACFW online critique group that got me started on this journey: Valerie Goree, Marcia Lahti, and the late Loretta Boyett (passed on to Glory, but never forgotten). Without your input, my writing would not be nearly as effective.

Eva Marie Everson – my mentor/instructor with Christian Writers' Guild. You took a timid, untrained student and turned her into a writer. Many thanks!

SincNE, and the folks who coordinate the Crimebake Writing Conference. I have attended many writing conferences, but without a doubt, Crimebake is one of the best. The workshops, seminars, panels, critiques, and every tiny aspect are well-executed, professional, and educational.

Special thanks to Hank Phillippi Ryan, Halle Ephron, and Roberta Isleib for your encouragement and spot-on critiques of my work.

Paula Proofreader (https://paulaproofreader.wixsite.com/home): I'm so glad I found you! My work is cleaner because of your eagle eye. Any mistakes are completely mine.

A heartfelt thank you to my brothers, Jack Shenton and Douglas Shenton, and my sister, Susan Shenton Greger for being enthusiastic cheerleaders during my writing journey. Your support means more than you'll know.

My husband, Wes, deserves special kudos for understanding my need to write. Thank you for creating my writing room – it's perfect, and I'm thankful for it every day. Thank you for your willingness to accept a house that's a bit cluttered, laundry that's not always done, and meals on the go. I love you.

And finally, to God be the glory. I thank Him for giving me the gift of writing and the inspiration to tell stories that shine the light on His goodness and mercy.

A Lesson in Love

Other Titles by this Author

Romance
Love's Harvest, Wartime Brides, Book 1
Love's Rescue, Wartime Brides, Book 2
Love's Belief, Wartime Brides, Book 3
Love's Allegiance, Wartime Brides, Book 4

Spies & Sweethearts, Sisters in Service, Book 1
The Mechanic & The MD, Sisters in Service, Book 2
The Widow & The War Correspondent, Sisters in Service, Book 3

Gold Rush Bride Hannah, Gold Rush Brides, Book 1
Gold Rush Bride Caroline, Gold Rush Brides, Book 2
Gold Rush Bride Tegan, Gold Rush Brides, Book 2

Dinah's Dilemma, Westward Home & Hearts Mail Order Brides
Rayne's Redemption, Westward Home & Hearts Mail Order Brides
Daria's Duke, Westward Home & Hearts Mail Order Brides
Ellie's Escape, Westward Home & Hearts Mail Order Brides
Beryl's Bounty Hunter, Westward Home & Hearts Mail Order Brides
Ivy's Inheritance, Westward Home & Hearts Mail Order Brides

Vanessa's Replacement Valentine, Brides of Pelican Rapids
A Family for Hazel, Brides of Pelican Rapids

Legacy of Love, Keepers of the Light

A Bride for Seamus, Proxy Bride Series
A Bride for Keegan, Proxy Bride Series

Estelle's Endeavor, Thanksgiving Books & Blessings Series, Collection 5
Francine's Foibles, Thanksgiving Books & Blessings Series, Collection 6

Maeve's Pledge, The Suffrage Spinsters Series

A Lesson in Love

Dial V for Valentine, You're On the Air Series
Dial S for Second Chances, You're On the Air Series

Love and Chocolate, The Chocolate Chronicles

Love at First Flight
Love Found in Sherwood Forest
On the Rails: A Harvey Girls Story
A Love Not Forgotten
A Doctor in the House
War's Unexpected Gift

Mystery
Under Fire, Ruth Brown Mystery Series, Book 1
Under Cover, Ruth Brown Mystery Series, Book 2
Under Ground, Ruth Brown Mystery Series, Book 3

Murder of Convenience, Women of Courage, Book 1
Murder at Madison Square Garden, Women of Courage, Book 2

Non-Fiction
WWII Word Find, Volume 1

Let's Connect!

www.LindaShentonMatchett.com

www.facebook.com/LindaShentonMatchettAuthor

www.pinterest.com/lindasmatchett

www.linkedin.com/in/authorlindamatchett

https://www.goodreads.com/author_linda_matchett

https://www.bookbub.com/authors/linda-shenton-matchett

Interested in more historical fiction?
Visit http://www.lindashentonmatchett.com/p/books.html

A Lesson in Love

www.ingramcontent.com/pod-product-compliance
Lightning Source LLC
LaVergne TN
LVHW041942070526
838199LV00051BA/2874